THE DARK MAN SPEAKS:

"Ages ago a particular creature—man—
was selected to develop into the dominant
life form on this planet. The agents of
mankind's development sought the evolution of
an environment suitable to themselves.
They devised the human race as a planoforming
agent, designed and programmed so perfectly
that it would not only create the environment
they desired but would self-destruct when it
was completed. They have always been wary
of prodigies, prophets, possible mutations,
who might redirect the course of events in
undesirable directions. They have dealt with
hundreds of philosophers and scientific
thinkers, killed or ruined, or backed and
assisted them, depending on whether these men
would aid their ends or mankind's survival.

"I have fought them for ages. Now you, too,
must fight, Dennis Guise. For the end draws
near, and if we fail, mankind will pay
the final price. . . ."

Great Science Fiction from SIGNET

BRIDGE OF ASHES

by
Roger Zelazny

A SIGNET BOOK
NEW AMERICAN LIBRARY

For Sally Turner
and
Sally Albaugh

NAL BOOKS ARE AVAILABLE AT QUANTITY DISCOUNTS
WHEN USED TO PROMOTE PRODUCTS OR SERVICES. FOR
INFORMATION PLEASE WRITE TO PREMIUM MARKETING DIVISION,
NEW AMERICAN LIBRARY, 1633 BROADWAY,
NEW YORK, NEW YORK 10019.

SIGNET TRADEMARK REG. U.S. PAT. OFF. AND FOREIGN COUNTRIES
REGISTERED TRADEMARK—MARCA REGISTRADA
HECHO EN WINNIPEG, CANADA

SIGNET, SIGNET CLASSIC, MENTOR, PLUME, MERIDIAN AND NAL BOOKS
are published by New American Library,
1633 Broadway, New York, New York 10019

First Signet Printing, July, 1976

3   4   5   6   7   8   9   10   11

PRINTED IN CANADA

Part I

I—
Day was the—
It—
. . . Saw the man, is—
. . . Man is moving through the woods. With him a band of others, hunters all. They are clad in the skins of animals. They bear sharpened sticks, fire-hardened. Mine is tipped with stone and decorated with a tracery of lines, inscribed with the point of the flint knife which hangs from the strip of leather about my—his waist. He wears leaves in his hair, and a shining object hangs from a thong about his throat. It is a thing of power which he had brought with him from the land of spirits beneath the sea. He leads the men in the hunt, raven-haired father's father of them all. His dark eyes describe the circuit of the beast. Silent, nostrils flaring, the others walk in his track. The air bears a sometime hint of the salt and the wrack, of the not-too-distant shores of that great water, mother of us all. He raises his hand and the men come to a halt.

He gestures again and they draw up on either side of him, crouching, spreading into a forward-curving arc. Then, once again, they halt.

He moves. He adjusts his grip on the haft of his weapon. Then, suddenly, his hands are empty. There comes a roar of pain from the glade before him. At this, the others rush forward, their spears held ready. The man draws his knife and follows.

He reaches the wounded beast—fallen and panting now, three of their shafts protruding from its side—in time to cut its throat. A cry goes up about him as the

3

quick slashing movement is executed. The weapons are withdrawn from the carcass. The stealth of the hunt is gone, replaced by words and laughter. The man moves to dress their prize, dividing most of the flesh for transport, retaining some for the victory meal which is now at hand.

The firemaker gathers tinder. Another fetches him dead limbs for fuel. Someone begins a nonmelodic song, a recitation with a lilt. The sun pushes its way toward the treetops. Small flowers unfold among the roots, the rocks, the fallen timber. There comes another whiff of the sea.

As the man skewers chunks of the flesh and passes these to the firemaker, he pauses for a moment in mid-gesture and rests his fingertips upon the shining object he wears. It seems a trifle warm to his touch. The moment passes. He shrugs. He hands the meat to the other. He moves to cut more.

There comes a sound—a deep, drawn-out hooting, breaking into a long, rising note which grows into a whistle, passes then beyond the audible, cuts a wake of vibration, showing that somewhere, strongly, it persists.

After a time, this subsides and the hooting begins once more—louder, nearer. It is accompanied by a distant crashing and crackling, as of the passage of a heavy body amid the shrubs, the trees.

The man places his hands on the ground and feels the vibrations within it. He rises to his feet.

"Go!" he says to the others, and he takes up his spear. "Now! Leave the food! Hurry!"

They obey him, fleeing the kill, the fire, leaving the man there alone.

When they have departed, the man begins his retreat from the wood. The notes of the challenge have run through yet another cycle and the forest still echoes with the sound of their passage.

When the hooting comes again, it is with such force and volume that it is felt as much as heard. The man hurries toward the meadow his party had crossed earlier. There had been a rocky knoll in its midst. . . .

He breaks into the open, running toward the hillock.

4

From the thunder at his back, he is already aware that he will be unable to attain a sufficient vantage in time to roll rocks down upon his pursuer.

He races toward a stony cleft, slips within it and turns, crouching.

The reflected sunlight dazzles his eyes, bouncing and dancing on the countless scales of its long, lithe body, flat tail, crooked limbs, horned head. It plows deep furrows in the meadow as, belly low, legs splaying, it propels itself with an awful power directly toward him. Neither sapling nor boulder causes it to swerve from its course. The tree is splintered, goes down, vanishes beneath it. Its head turns from side to side as its horns encounter the stone. The boulder begins to move, almost imperceptibly at first; the stone is rocking, more and more of its damp underside exposed at each teetering shift; it is cast, rolling off to the left, with a final toss of that sea-wet thick neck, sun-rich and throbbing with a great new hooting shriek, blasting dust and gravel before it, continuing the sidewise swimming strokes which bury each limb in the earth as they drive it on.

The man braces the butt of his spear against the stone. He searches that blazing body for some flaw, some imperfection, some weakness. He makes his decision and aligns the point of his weapon. He squints against the blown dust. His ears ache from that high-pitched cry. He waits.

Moments later, his spear is shattered and the rocks about him are shaken by the impact. He flattens himself against the rear of the crevice as a horn drives toward him. The horn stops inches short of his belly.

Now, it begins to throw its weight from side to side, spatulate legs continuing their paddlelike movement, body ringing like a great bell each time that it strikes against the stone. The man smells the dried brine upon its armored hide. He is nearly deafened by the new cry it emits. He stabs at its tossing head, but his flint blade is broken in his hand. He feels the rocks shudder again. He clutches at his amulet, now burning hot upon his breast.

The next thrust penetrates his side, and we scream as we are impaled and lifted—thrown. . . .

Pain and breaking. Blackness and pain. Blackness. Light. Has the sun moved higher? We are wet with our own bright blood. The beast is gone. We are going. Here, alone, among the grasses . . . Insects circle us, walk upon us, drink of us. A jagged mount of bone has risen from the continent of my body, snow-capped. . . . I—

Blackness.

The man awakens to the sound of their wailing. They have returned to him, his children. They have brought her with them, and she cradles his head in her lap, weeping. She has strewn him with herbs and flowers and wrapped him in a bright garment. He smiles to her and she touches his brow. His amulet has grown cold. His awareness begins to fade once more. He closes his eyes, and above him she begins to sing the long lament. At this, the others turn and move away, leaving them there alone. There is love. We—

I—

There is a flash of blue, a circle of white. . . .

The beast has returned to its place.

And of self the—

—to old be. Was the—

. . . Man by the seaside. See—

. . . Drawing is the man in the damp sand. Power. His eye the binder of angles. His I— Opposite and adjacent, of course. Where the line cuts them. At hand, the sea forms green steps and trellises, gentle, beneath the warm blue sky; gentle and unnoticed, as he scribes the circle. For seventy-some years has he known the sea near Syracuse, here in Sicily. He had never been far from this sea, even in the days of his studies in Alexandria. It is not surprising then that he can ignore its wash, splash, spray, its plays of light and color. Clean sea, living sea, a touch of deafness and a totality of concentration, and the sea is as distant and abstract as all the grains of sand he reckoned to fill the universe, displaced about all bodies within it in accordance

6

with the law he had determined in the matter of the purity of the King's crown, that day he ran naked from his bath shouting he had found it. . . . The sea and the sigh of the sea at the side of the sea . . . Now, now very few things matter but the relationships between forms. The pulleys, the pumps, the levers, all of them clever and useful in their time. But Syracuse has fallen. Too many Romans this time even for the mirror-trick. And does it really matter? The ideas outlive their embodiments. The ingenious devices were only toys, really, flitting shadows of the principles he had cast for with nets of thought. Now, now . . . This one . . . If a relationship between things, between events, could be expressed in a great number of small steps . . . How many? Many . . . ? Few . . . ? Any. Any number desired. And if there were a boundary of some sort . . . Yes. A . . . A limit. Yes. Then up to that point, any number of steps . . . As we had done with π and the polygons. Only now let us take it a step further. . . .

He does not see the shadow of the man on the sand to his left. The thoughts, the deafness, the promise of the Roman commander Marcellus that he would not be harmed . . . He does not see, he does not hear the question. Again. Look up, old man! We must answer! The blade comes out of the scabbard, and again there are words. Respond! Respond! He traces another circle, idly, thinking the steps of change within limits, groping for the new vocabulary its expression will require—

The stroke!

We are pierced. We fall forward. . . . Why? Let me—

My eyes fall upon that final circle. There is a soft blue all about it. Not of the sea, the sky . . . There is—

Now, now, now . . . The pain, the waste of it all . . .

I, Flavius Claudius Julianus, he thinks, pacifier of Gaul, Emperor of Rome, last defender of the old gods, pass now as they have passed. Pity, Lord of the lightnings, and thou, shaker of the earth and tamer of horses, and thou, lady of the grain fields, and thou,

7

thou . . . all ye other lords and ladies of high Olympus . . . pity, pity, pity that I could not have served you better, oh lovers and holders of the world and its trees and grasses and wet holy places, and all things fleet and crawling, flying and burrowing, all that move, breathe, touch, sing and cry. . . . I could have served you better had I stayed at Ctesiphon, laying siege to that great city, than cross the Tigris to seek King Sapor in this waste. For here I die. This wounding's mortal, and all the Persian army rings us round. Hot, dry, desolate land . . . Fitting. A place like this perhaps, where the Galilean went to be tempted . . . Is this irony necessary, new Lord? You have wrested the earth from its keepers to throw it away. . . . It is another world you claim to lead them to. . . . You care no more for the green, the brown, the gold, the glades, the glens, than this dry, hot place of rock and sand . . . and of death. What is death to you? A gateway . . . To me it is more than my end, for I have failed. . . . You slay me as the children of Constantine took my kin. . . . For yours this may be a gateway, for me it is the end. . . . I see where my blood pools. . . . I give it to the Earth— Gaea, old mother. . . . I have fought and I have finished. . . . Old ones, I am thine—

The blood's red ring is bleached. About it, for an instant, a blueness. A roaring seems to begin. He. He. He . . . I—

Tell me if anything is ever done. . . . This then, I—

He stares from the window, sorting the motions of the birds. Spring has come to Rome. But the sun is falling and the shadows lengthen. He sorts the colors, the shades, the textures. Had I this city to build, I would have done differently. . . . He regards the clouds. But then it might never have been done. . . . He leans his head back against the wall, runs his fingers through his beard, tugs at his lower lip. There were so many things. . . . To fly, to go beneath the seas, to build palaces and marvelous devices, to channel rivers, to plumb all the laws of nature, to merge the scientific and the esthetic, striving perpetually within me, getting in each

8

other's ways ... Yet there were many things done for Ludovico, only all of them trifles. ... The Great Horse ... He would have liked to have seen that carried to completion. Sad, how the opportunities invariably arose at the wrong times. Or if things did seem to be going right, that something always came to cancel them. So many things that might be of use. It is as if the world resists. ... And now ... The Magnificent Giuliano de' Medici dead this March past ... There is little to hold me here now, and this new French king has spoken of the manor of Cloux, near Amboise, a pleasant place— and no duties. ... Perhaps the rest would be good, to think, to pursue my studies. I may even paint a little. ...

He turns from the window, retreats. There is a white circle on that field of blue, though the moon is not yet risen. He might— I—

Tell me if anything is ever done. ...

... And she sings the lament as he lies bleeding.

The beast is returned to the sea. She brushes away insects. She cradles his head in her lap. There is no movement. He does not seem to breathe.

Yet some warmth is in him still. ...

She finds more words. ... Trees and mountains, streams and plains, how can this thing be? He whose sons and sons' sons have hunted among you since before the hills were made ... He who has spoken with the powers beneath the sea ... How can he pass as men have passed into the land of dreams? Rend yourselves, hide yourselves, spill yourselves over, weep ... if the son of the land can walk it no more.

Her voice carries across the meadow, is lost among the trees. ... Pain, pain, pain ... I—

Drunk again. Who cares? Perhaps I am as worthless as they say, a dirty Swiss madman. ... I saw and I spoke. It is they who are mad, who do not listen. ... Yet ... Nothing I have said has been taken right. Suppose it is always to be so? Suppose ... Damn Voltaire! He knew what I meant. He knew I never intended that

9

we all go live in the woods! Out to show his wit at the price of an idea . . . Natural, within society, is what I said—over and again. . . . Only in society can man have knowledge of good and evil. In nature he is merely innocent. He knew! I'll swear he knew, damned mocker! And damn all popularizers of a man's work! The perversity of costumed dandies playing at the simple . . . Thérèse! I miss you tonight. . . . Where is that bottle? There . . . Seek goodness and God and order in nature and in the heart . . . and in the bottle, I should have added. The room swims well tonight. There are times—damn these moments—when it all seems worthless, all, all that I have done and all else in this mad world. Who cares? At times, I seem to see so clearly. . . . But . . . The faith of a Savoyard Vicar is not mine tonight. . . . There have been times when I feared that I was truly mad, times else when I doubted some thought or other. . . . Now I fear that it does not matter whether I am mad or sane, right or wrong. Does not matter in the least. My words are cast into the Föhn, strewn, effectless, gone. . . . The wind blows on, the world goes as it will, coursing the same route it would have taken had I never been at all. . . . *Bacche, benevenies gratus et optatus, per quem noster animus fit letificatus*. . . . It does not matter that I saw and spoke. It does not matter that those who scorned me may be right. It does not matter. . . .

Head resting on outflung arm, he regards the bottom of the bottle. We see it go white in the flickering light, and all around it blue. . . . We spin. We—

I—

Aiee! she cries, shaking, the lament done, the blood drying, the body still and pale. And again, as she throws herself upon him and clings to the once-warm form. Air rushes from my lungs with a noise like a sob. The pain!

The pain . . .

. . . But there is nothing left. My hopes—the dreams of a fool . . . I welcomed this thing when it came.

10

The old order, into which I, Marie Jean Antoine Nicholas Caritat, was born Marquis de Condorcet, had had its day and darkened it Long ago had I seen that, and I welcomed the Revolution. But three years past was I seated in the Legislative Assembly. And the terror . . . But one year past, because I favored Gironde, did I fall from grace and flee the Jacobins. . . . Laughable. Here I sit, their prisoner. I know what must come next, and they shall not have it of me. Laughable—for still do I believe. . . . Everything I said in the *Sketch* . . . That man may one day be free from want and war, that the increase and the spread of knowledge, the discovery of the laws of social behavior, may bring man toward perfection . . . Laughable—to believe this and plot to cheat the guillotine this way . . . Yet, moderation is not the way of revolution, a thing we humanists who get involved often learn too late. . . . I still believe, yet these things seem farther off than once they did. . . . Let us hope that that is all there is to it. . . . I am weary. The entire business tedious . . . I find that I am of no further use here. . . . It is time to write an ending and close the book. . . .

We make the final preparations. At the moment of pain, I—he . . . We see through a blue haze dimly a pale circle upon the wall. . . .

Now, now again, ever and always . . . The pain and the broken body she clutches, breathing into the mouth, beating upon my breast, rubbing his hands and neck . . . As if by this to call back, as if by this to share her spirit in her breath . . .

The ground is sharp beneath our shoulders, and there is pain as the breath rattles forth. . . . The blood will flow if I move again. He must stay very still. . . . The sun drops spears upon our eyelids. . . .

. . . Gilbert Van Duyn cast a final glance over his speech. A crutch, he thought. I already know what I am going to say, know exactly where I might depart from the text, and how. . . . Not really that important. The thing is already distributed. All I have to do is get

11

up and say the words. Still . . . Addressing the General Assembly of the United Nations is hardly the same as talking to a classroom full of students. I was less nervous in Stockholm, that day, eight years ago. . . . Strange, that the Prize means so much. . . . Without it, someone else would be reading this—or something very like it. . . . And it probably would not have made that much difference. . . . The main thing is to get it said. . . . He ran his hand through what remained of his hair. How *will* the voting go, I wonder? They all say it should be close. . . . I just hope the ones we are concerned about can take a longer view, be willing to see beyond the surface inequities. . . . God! I really hope so. . . .

The speaker was nearing the end of his introduction. A soft undercurrent of murmurs the texture of half a hundred tongues still flowed across the hall, fading as the moments ticked by. Soon, soon now . . . He glanced at the speaker, the clock on the wall, his own hands. . . .

The speaker concluded, turned his head, gestured. Gilbert Van Duyn rose and moved to the microphone. He smiled as he placed the papers before him. A momentary pause . . . He began to speak. . . .

Dead silence.

Not only the murmuring, but every small sound within the hall had ceased. Not a cough nor the scraping of a chair, not the rattle of a briefcase nor the scratch of a match; not a rustle of paper, the clink of a water tumbler, the closing of a door nor the sound of a footstep. Nothing.

Gilbert Van Duyn paused and looked up.

Nor was there any movement.

Total stillness, as in a snapshot . . . Not a body stirred. Cigarette smoke hung motionless in the air.

He turned his head, seeking some small activity— anything—within the assembly.

His eyes passed over the figure within the tableau several times before the expression and the stance registered, before the object clasped in both hands and thrust forward came suddenly to his notice.

12

Then he froze.

The man, in the delegation from one of the smaller, warmer nations, had obviously sprung to his feet but a moment before—his chair still tilted backward, an upset folder still hanging at an impossible angle before him, spilling still papers into the air.

The man held a pistol, pointed directly at him, a thin wisp of unmoving smoke twisted to the left of its muzzle.

Slowly then, Gilbert Van Duyn moved. He left his notes, drew away from the microphone, stepped down, crossed back, made his way toward the place where the man stood with the pistol, eyes narrowed, teeth bared, brows tightened.

When he came up beside him, he stood for a moment, then reached out cautiously, touched the man's arm.

. . . Stiff, unyielding, statuelike. It did not feel like flesh beneath his fingers, but some substance much denser, more rigid. But then, even the cloth of the sleeve felt stiffer than it should have.

Turning, he touched the next nearest man. The sensations were the same. Even the shirtfront behaved as if it were of a coarse, heavily starched material.

Gilbert Van Duyn regarded the papers, still unnaturally suspended before the gunman. He touched one. The same rigidity . . . He tugged at it. It cracked soundlessly.

He extracted an automatic pencil from a delegate's pocket, held it before him, released it. It hung in the air, motionless.

He glanced at his watch. The second hand was not moving. He shook it, put it to his ear. Nothing.

Returning to the gunman, he sighted along the barrel of the pistol. There could be no doubt. It was aimed directly at the spot he had recently vacated.

. . . And what was that up ahead?

He straightened, made his way forward, regarded the pellet about six feet out from the muzzle. It was the bullet, almost hanging there, creeping forward at a barely perceptible velocity.

13

He shook his head, stepped back.

Suddenly, it became necessary that he know the extent of the phenomenon. He turned and headed for the door, his pace increasing as he went. Passing through, he moved to the nearest window and regarded the world beyond.

Traffic stood silent and still, birds hovered in midflight, not a flag rippled. There was no motion to the clouds. . . .

"Spooky, isn't it?" something like a voice seemed to say. "Necessary, though. I realized at—you might say, the last minute—that I had to talk with you."

Van Duyn turned.

A dark man, clad in green slacks and a pale sport shirt, was leaning against the wall, left foot resting on a large black satchel. Stockily built, wide forehead, dark eyes, heavy brows, flaring nostrils . . . He was uncertain as to the swarthy man's race or nationality.

"Yes," Van Duyn answered, "it is spooky. You know what's happened?"

The other nodded.

"As I said, I wanted to talk with you."

"So you stopped time?"

Something like laughter. Then, "Just the opposite. I've speeded you up. You may grow extremely hungry in what seems like the next few minutes. Just tell me when you do. I have food with me." He hefted the satchel. "Come this way, please."

"You are not really talking," Van Duyn said. "I just realized that. Your words are coming directly into my head."

The man nodded again.

"It's this or write notes. Listen! You can't even hear your footsteps. Sound is a trifle slow at the moment— or rather, we are too fast for it Come on. Time is a dear commodity."

He turned, and Van Duyn followed him out of the building. He took what seemed an unnecessarily long time to open the door.

Then he seized Van Duyn's hand and did something with the satchel. They rose into the air.

Moments later, they had come to rest atop the building. The man turned then and gestured at the East River, a piece of muddy glass, and at the hazed and grainy sky where strands of smoke lay like bloated things on a beach.

"There is that," he said. "And here . . ." He took him by the arm and led him to the other end of the roof. ". . . the city."

Van Duyn looked out, across the silent city where the still cars lay at the bottom of the sea of their exhausts—pedestrians, storefronts, flagpoles, hydrants, shrubbery, benches, signs, tangles of wire, lightpoles, grass, a few trees and a stray cat all embedded within it. He looked up at dark clouds, down at the play of light and shade on dingy surfaces.

"What is it that you want me to see?" he asked.

"There is pollution," said the other.

"I am well aware of that—particularly today."

". . . and power, and beauty."

"I can't deny it."

"The resolution you were about to urge be passed . . . What do you think its chances really are?"

"Everyone feels the voting will be close."

The dark man nodded.

"Yet what is it basically?" he said. "A thing which would put some pressure on those nations not party to them to become signatory to several already existing treaties dealing with contamination of the seas and the atmosphere. Everyone agrees in principle that the world should be kept clean, yet there is strong resistance to the measures proposed."

"But understandable," Van Duyn said. "The wealthy, powerful nations owe their power, their wealth, their standards of existence, to the sort of exploitation the others are now being called upon to forgo—and the call comes just at the point when those others are approaching a position where they can indulge in the same sorts of enterprise and reap similar benefits. It is only human for them to feel cheated, see it as a neocolonial conspiracy, resist it."

"Only human," said the other. "That, unfortunately,
15

is the problem—and it is a much larger problem than you could possibly realize. I respect you, enormously, Dr. Van Duyn, and because of this I have decided to take this time to tell you exactly what that word means. Human. Do you think Leakey and the others were right, that it was East Africa where some hominid first took his thumb and got a grip on the humanity business?"

"It is quite possible. We may never know for certain, but there is evidence—"

"I will spare you the trouble. The answer is yes. That is where they did it. But they were not entirely unassisted in the matter—at that point, and at many other points far earlier in time."

"I do not understand. . . ."

"Of course not. Your education was based on admirable presumptions of regularity and an unavoidable eschewal of the teleological. You are a victim of your own sound thinking. There is no way you could have arrived at the proper conclusions, short of being told. Yet the answer is teleological: the human race was designed to serve a particular end, and that end is now in sight."

"Mad! Ridiculous!" Van Duyn said, and the dark man gestured toward the city.

"Can you make things move again?" he asked.

Van Duyn lowered his head.

"Then hear me out. Suspend judgment until I have finished the story. Are you hungry?"

"Yes."

The other reached into his satchel.

"Sandwiches, wine, lemonade, chocolate, coffee . . ." He unfolded a cloth and spread the food upon it. "Eat, and listen."

"Ages ago," he began, "a particular creature was selected to develop into the dominant life form on this planet. It was given certain breaks and certain challenges, all of which, when utilized or overcome, marked it indelibly with particular traits as it moved along the road to a higher sentience. Its course was directed through many of the situations recently determined by archaeologists and anthropologists to lead up to the hominids and beyond, to bring about the dominance of this planet by the gregarious killer ape. It was necessary to produce a life form of this sort which would achieve a communal existence and acquire the ability to manipulate its environment in such a fashion as to give eventual rise to an urban life style and an inevitable state of high industrial development."

Van Duyn shook his head, but his mouth was full and he had no choice but to listen as the other went on:

"This was desirable solely because of the physical alteration of the world which would come about as a by-product of such a civilization's normal functioning. The agents of mankind's development sought the evolution of an environment characterized by the presence of such compounds as sulfur dioxide, nitrogen oxide, methyl mercury, fluorocarbons 11 and 12, tetrachloroethylene, carbon tet, carbon monoxide, polychlorinated biphenyls, organic phosphates and numerous other industrial effluents and discharges which characterize the modern world. In short, they devised the human race as a planoforming agent, designed and programmed so perfectly that it would not only do this job for them, but would self-destruct when it was completed."

"But why?" asked Van Duyn. "What purpose would this serve?"

"The human race," said the other, "was so designed by beings from another world. I do not know what events finally destroyed their own planet, though I can make some obvious guesses. A few of them escaped and came here. The Earth apparently filled the bill as a suitable world, if certain changes could be effected. There were too few of them to set about the massive job, so they assured the development of the human species to do it for them. They have been sleeping all this while, in stasis chambers aboard their vessels. Periodically, one of them is awakened to monitor the human race's progress and to make whatever adjustments

17

may be required to keep things moving along the proper track."

"Toward our destruction?"

"Yes. They have calculated things pretty closely—possibly having had experience with this sort of situation before—so that the planet becomes suitable for them at just about the point where it becomes uninhabitable for humanity. Your purpose is to do the job for them and expire at its completion."

"How could such a type of being have evolved? I cannot understand the natural development of a creature adapted to a planet despoiled in such a sophisticated fashion. Unless—"

The other shrugged. "—unless they are some secondary species evolved on an already ruined world? Or the primary one, struck by a fortuitous run of mutations? Or perhaps they were far enough along in the life sciences to induce the changes to save themselves after they had already wrecked their world? I do not know. I only know that they seek a particular sort of post-ecological-catastrophe environment and that they are well on their way to achieving it here."

"You said that they keep us under surveillance, and make—adjustments?"

"Yes."

"This would seem to indicate that our programming to achieve their ends is not perfect."

"True. For the past several thousand years they have been keeping a much closer watch over human society than they had previously. They have always been wary of prodigies, prophets, possible mutations, who might redirect the course of events in undesirable directions. Their impact could be greater now than, say, ten thousand years ago. Also, statistically, the possibility of their occurrence has increased. Consequently, they were much more alert during this time to stifle premature technological developments which might have slowed or thwarted their program, and to discourage philosophical tendencies which could have had similar effects. On the other hand, they encouraged the opposite. For an example, they saw an advantage

18

in promoting the otherworldly aspects of Christianity, Buddhism and Islam for purposes of minimizing the importance of the Earth itself. They have dealt with hundreds of philosophers, scientific thinkers—"

"Dealt with?"

"Killed or ruined, or backed and assisted—as the case may be."

"It is a terrible picture that you paint," said Van Duyn. "Why have you told me all these things?"

The dark man looked away, out over the city, fingering a medallion he wore about his neck.

"I have fought them," he finally said, "for ages. At best, I might have succeeded in slowing things a bit. Now, though, our struggle is rushing to a conclusion— the conclusion toward which they directed the race so long ago. I am not certain how much of a chance remains. It would almost seem necessary to effect some change in the nature of man in order to defeat them. What or how, I do not know. What I am attempting now is to buy time, to slow things as much as possible, while I continue to search for an answer. The passage of the resolution now before the General Assembly would help in this—considerably. I was aware that the voting would run very close. This is why I arranged for a spectacle—your assassination. I felt that with the endorsement of a martyr, its chances of passage would be considerably improved. At the last moment, however, I realized that my respect, my fondness for you, would not permit me to proceed quite so coldbloodedly. I owed you this much of explanation. By then, though, it was too late to stop the assassin. And unnecessary. While no one has ever succeeded in controlling time, that bridge of ashes man leaves behind him, I possess the ability to manipulate a person's physiology to the point where the effect is the same as a time-stoppage. So I did this, to give you this explanation, to give you a choice."

"A choice?"

The other nodded.

"I am capable of using almost anyone. Almost . . ."

19

"I see," said Van Duyn. "I also see that my death could make the difference. . . . Who are you, anyway?"

The dark man shook his head.

"There is simply no time to tell you my story, as it is longer than all of history. As for names . . . I have lost count of them. You might say I am an early experiment of theirs that went bad. And I managed to steal a few things from them before they caught up with me. They make periodic attempts to destroy me and my woman, but they have never been able to recall our lives entirely. They were handicapped in many ways by the uncongenial environment—and over the ages we have acquired many defenses. I am . . . their adversary. That is all. That is enough."

"All right," said Van Duyn, straightening. He glanced out over the city once more, turned, crossed the roof and regarded the dark river. "All right."

After a time, he turned away and looked at the dark man.

"Take me back down."

The other reached into his satchel. Moments later, he took his hand. They left the roof.

Below, they entered the building. Van Duyn headed toward the assembly hall. He looked back once, to say something to the dark man, and discovered that the other was no longer with him.

He continued on, entering the hall, moving back along the aisle he had previously followed. He paused beside the man with the pistol, studying his contorted face. He checked the position of the bullet, which had advanced considerably in his absence. Then he remounted the podium, returned to the lectern.

He reached for his notes, took them into his hand. He glanced up then at the United Nations flag, blue, with the white circle of the world at its center. From the corner of his eye, he seemed to detect a movement. Then something struck and we— He— I—

Slumped across the lectern now, he— We regard the white circle on the field of blue as everything else grows dim and—

He— I—

I . . . I am— I.
I!
I am! I am! I am!

. . . He lies there, breathing gently. The bleeding
has stopped. It is night, and she has built a fire and
covered him over with the skins of animals. He has
been very cold. She has brought him water in a large
shell. I begin to understand.

Part II

Richard Guise walked in the hills, beheading flowers with a stick. Northern New Mexico is an extraordinary bump on the Earth and summer brings it to its clement best. But Richard Guise had no eye for scenery that day. His vision was turned in upon himself.

He descended into an arroyo, followed it to a place where it branched, then stood undecided. Finally, he sighed and seated himself on a stone in the shade of the farther wall, sat tracing patterns in the dust.

"Damn!" he said, after a time, and again, "Damn!"

Richard Guise resembled the countryside in some ways, though he had been born forty-some years before in urban New Jersey: heavy-set, well-tanned; hair a mix of sand and gray, darker across the backs of the big-knuckled hands that guided his stick; dark eyes wide of a once-broken nose.

But he was not fond of the mountains, the piñons, the rocks, the cacti, the cottonwoods. He was President of the International Telepathic Operators Union, and despite the enormous efficiencies of twenty-first-century communication, of which he was a significant part, he would have felt far more comfortable in a large urban environment, preferably Eastern. He maintained offices in such locations, true, but his was the same problem which had caused all telepaths with young children to seek residence in remote areas. Only, with Dennis, something had gone wrong. . . .

He reached with his special sense, down into the infra-awareness of a stinkbug picking its way among pebbles.

. . . A world of coarse texture and massive forms, of striking odors and peculiar kinesthetic sensations . . .

He swung his stick and observed the sensations dwindle to nothing, the kinesthetics fading last. It was not at all true that empathy bred sympathy. Sometimes the best thing about a channel of experience was the ability to cut it off.

These walks had become more frequent in recent weeks, as it became increasingly apparent that something was still wrong with their son. Beyond the fatigue factor and the possibility of broadcasting his feelings near the child, he simply did not like shielding his thoughts around Vicki. He had to get off somewhere to think them, though.

"Damn!"

He stirred the mashed beetle into the sand, smoothed it over, glanced at his watch. Perhaps the doctor would have something good to say this time.

Victoria Guise tended her plants. She watered, misted, cultivated; she plucked off dead leaves, added nutriments, shifted pots from courtyard to patio, windowsill to bench, sunlight to shade and vice versa; she fondled them with her thoughts. Blue shorts, white halter, red bandana, leather sandals, hung, clung, wrapped her thin, pepper-haired, five-and-a-half-foot, randomly mole-flecked person. Whenever she was particularly troubled the plants received more than usual attention. Green eyes squinted, she sought and dealt with burn, droop, dryness, mold, wither and insect depredation. She was aware that this was a piece of emotional misdirection. Even so, it was generally effective.

For now, she did not have to shield her thoughts and feelings. Except— It was taking much longer than she had anticipated. The doctor was still in with Dennis, and Dick would probably be returning before much longer. If only— She decided that the impatiens could use a little more light, and the navy petunias still looked thirsty. She returned to the tap.

As she was pinching back the asparagus fern, a faint, inquiring thought reached her: *Is it all right?* She felt Dick's presence, sensed the landscape through which he moved, dry, rocky, house up on the hill ahead. He was passing along the small arroyo to the north.

I do not know, she replied. *He is still in there with him.*

Oh.

She felt him slow his pace, caught a whisper of his feelings.

It cannot be too much longer, she added.

I would not think so.

Several minutes later, she heard a door close inside the house.

Hurry, she sent suddenly.

What is it?

I—I think he is finished.

All right. A sense of their house, nearer.

She passed through the gate, closing it behind her, walked around to the south wall. Only marigolds here. They never seemed to need anything special. She inspected them.

"Mrs. Guise?"—faintly, Dr. Winchell's voice from within the house.

She paused, studying the flowers. Another moment or so . . .

"Mrs. Guise—Oh!"

Voices then from the courtyard. Conversation. Dick had returned. She sighed and moved back in that direction.

Entering, she glanced at her husband and the doctor, who had just seated themselves on the chairs near the geraniums. Dr. Winchell was a young, big man, florid, overweight. His straw-colored hair was already thinning, and he ran his fingers through it several times as they spoke.

"Mrs. Guise," he said, nodding, and he made as if to rise as she approached.

She seated herself on the bench across from them, and he eased back into his seat.

"I was just telling your husband," he said, "that it is simply too early to venture a prognosis, but—"

27

Let us have the bad of it straight, Dick interrupted.

Winchell nodded, glanced at Vicki. She inclined her head slightly, her eyes never leaving his own.

"All right," he said, declining the opportunity to switch away from the purely verbal. "It is not the most encouraging situation, but you must bear in mind that he is still a child—a very adaptable creature—and the fact that this relocation was to a spot as isolated—"

"Has he been permanently damaged?" Richard asked.

"I— It is impossible to answer that at this point. You have only been here a short while and—"

"How long until you can tell for certain?"

"Again, I can't answer you—"

"Is there anything you *can* tell me?"

"Richard," Vickie said. "Please . . ."

"It's all right," Winchell said. "Yes, as a matter of fact I can tell you more about what caused it."

"Go ahead."

"When I first saw Dennis, you lived over twenty miles from the nearest city—a good safety margin, based on accepted range figures for telepathic phenomena. At that distance, a telepathic child should have been sufficiently removed from the urban thought bombardment that he would remain unaffected. Dennis, however, exhibited all the signs of early reception reaction and retreated into catatonia. Neither of you were undergoing anxieties of the sort which might have induced this. At that time, it was suggested that some physical anomaly of the locale might have enhanced reception, or some nearer habitation be housing a broadcaster of thoughts exceptionally distressful to the child. So we recommended you relocate to an even remoter site and see whether the condition would clear up of its own accord."

Richard Guise nodded. "Six times now we've moved. For the same so-called reasons. The kid is thirteen years old. He doesn't talk, he doesn't walk. The nurse still changes his pants and bathes him. Everyone says an institution would be the worst thing, and I am still able to agree. But we have just moved again and nothing is different."

"Yes," Winchell said, "his condition has remained virtually unchanged. He is still suffering the effects of that initial trauma."

"Then the move was of no benefit whatever," Richard said.

"That is not what I said. Simple relocation could not alter what had already occurred. The purpose of the move was to avoid further exposure to adverse stimuli and to give the child's natural recuperative powers an opportunity to effect his return to some sort of equilibrium. It is apparently too early to see evidence of such recovery—"

"Or too late," Richard said.

"—but the move was certainly well advised," Winchell continued. "Just because our study of the few thousand known telepaths has provided certain norms, we should not accept them as gospel—not with a brand-new mutation in human stock. Not this early, not when so much still remains to be learned."

"Are you trying to say he was abnormal—even for a telepath—from the very beginning?"

Winchell nodded.

"Yes," he replied. "I have tried some recently developed tests, including an experiment in which two other telepaths were involved. I entered Dennis' mind and used his receptive abilities to reach them. The nearer is thirty miles from here, the second forty."

"Dennis picked up thoughts from forty miles away?"

"Yes, which explains his initial reception reaction. You were never that far removed from sources of trouble at your previous addresses. Here, though . . . Here, even with a forty-mile range, you have room to spare—plenty of it. His condition appears to be purely functional, and we do have numerous case histories from which to draw encouragement, dating from the days before the mutation was recognized."

"True, there is that," Richard said. "So . . . What do you recommend now?"

"I think we should have one of the new TP therapists come out and work with him—every day, for a while—to reorient him."

"I've read a bit about those early cases," Vicki said. "Sometimes the trauma was too strong and they never developed personalities of their own. . . . They just remained schizoid collections of the bits and pieces with which they had been imprinted. Others withdrew from everything and never—"

"There is no point in dwelling on the worst," Dr. Winchell said. "A good number recovered too, you know. You have already done a beneficial thing in bringing him here. Also, remember that the therapists know a lot more about the condition now than anyone did a generation ago—or even ten years back. Or five. Let's give it a chance. Try to think about the positive aspects. Remember how easily your attitudes, your feelings can be communicated."

Vicki nodded.

"Can you recommend a therapist?"

"Actually, I have several possibles in mind. I will have to check their availability. The best course of treatment would probably involve a therapist who could live in and work with him every day—at least for a while. I will investigate as soon as I get back and let you know—sometime tomorrow."

"All right," Richard said. "Tell them we have a nice guest room."

Winchell began to rise.

"We would like you to stay to dinner," Vicki said.

Winchell eased himself back down.

"I thank you."

Richard Guise smiled for the first time that day, rose to his feet.

"What are you drinking?"

"Scotch and soda."

He nodded and swung off toward the house.

"Forty miles . . ." he muttered.

Lydia Dimanche came to stay at the Guise house, a small, graceful woman with a musical voice and eyes which almost matched the black twists of her hair. They guessed that she might be Polynesian.

Lydia saw Dennis every day, feeding, channeling, directing, organizing sensory and extrasensory input. When she was not with Dennis she kept to herself, back in her room, down in town, up in the hills. She took her meals with the Guises, but never volunteered information concerning her patient. When asked directly, she normally replied that it was still too early to see clearly, to say anything for certain.

Months later, when Richard Guise departed on a lengthy business trip, Dennis' condition still seemed unchanged. The daily sessions went on. Vicki spent more and more time with her plants. The few minutes, mornings and afternoons, grew into hours. Evenings, she began reading gardening books; she obtained more plants, had a small greenhouse constructed.

One morning, Lydia emerged from Dennis' room to find the taller woman leaning against the wall.

"Victoria," she said, a beginning smile falling toward its opposite.

"I want to read him, Lydia. All this time . . . I have to see what he is like now "

"I have to advise against it. I have been controlling him quite strictly, and any intrusive thoughts or feelings might upset the balances I am trying to—"

"I am not going to broadcast. I just want to look."

"There is not really that much to see at this point. He will seem as he always has—"

"I have to see. I insist."

"You give me no choice," Lydia said, stepping aside. "But I wish you would think about it for a minute before you go in."

"I have already thought about it."

Vicki entered the room, moved to the side of the bed. Dennis lay on his side, staring past her at the far wall. His eyes did not move, not even when she passed directly before him.

She opened her mind and reached, very carefully, toward him.

Her eyes were dry when she emerged. She walked

past Lydia, through the front rooms and out into the courtyard. She seated herself on the bench and stared at the geraniums. She did not move when Lydia came and sat beside her.

For a long while, neither spoke.

Then, finally, Vicki said, "It's like giving isometrics to a corpse."

Lydia shook her head.

"It only seems that way," she said. "The fact that there are no obvious changes cannot be held as too important right now. At any time during the months to come, the exercises in which we are engaged could suddenly become crucial, making all the difference between stability and continued dysfunction. This is another reason I did not want you to check on him now. Your own morale is an important part of his environment."

"I had to see," Vicki said.

"I understand. But please do not do it again."

"I won't. I do not want to."

After a time, *I do not know about the morale part, though,* Vicki indicated. *I do not see how I can manage it. I do not know how to change responses, reactions—here, inside. I was afraid of things so much of the time. . . . When I was a child it was my sister Eileen. She was not TP; I could read her thoughts of me. Later there were teachers. Then the whole world . . . Going to hell in a handbasket . . . Then my first husband . . . Paul . . . Life was a lousy place till I met Dick. I wanted someone like him—older, stronger, who knew how to do all the things I could not do—to keep things safe, together. And he did, too. Before I met him, it always seemed as if the world was on the verge of falling apart all about me. He made the feeling go away—or kept it a good distance off. The same thing, I guess. I had felt there was nothing he could not do, that things would always be good with him. The world would work the way that it should. I would not be hurt. Then—this—happened—with Dennis. Now, I am afraid again. . . . It has been growing and growing ever since it happened. I watch the news and I remem-*

ber only the stories of breakdown, disaster, malfunction, pollution. I read, and I am impressed only by the bad parts of life. . . . Is it the world, or is it me? Or could it be both of us? Now Dick is gone away again and Dennis stays the same. . . . I do not know. I just do not know. . . .

Lydia put her arm about her shoulders.

You have looked and seen and you are afraid, she told her. *Fear is often a good thing. Despair is not. Fear can increase your awareness, strengthen your will to fight. Despair is withdrawal—*

But what is there to fight? And how do I fight it?

There is hope for Dennis. I would not persist in my efforts if I did not believe this. I could as easily be working on other cases where the results are more readily apparent. Yet, somewhere along the way, a therapist develops a feeling about a patient, about his chances for recovery. I have such a feeling here. I do not believe that it will be easy, or that it will occur soon. It may even take years, and it will be extremely difficult. But remember, I know him better than anyone else—even yourself—and I feel there is reason for you to have hope. You have had only a brief glimpse of that which is within him. I have seen more. As to your other fears, perhaps it is that there is some correspondence. At some level within yourself, it may be that the fragmentation of his developing personality is analogous to all the things which affected you so strongly until you met Richard. Perhaps Dennis seems the image of a schizoid world. The fact that Richard can do nothing to help him may have stirred up these other matters with the arousal of this anxiety. It is easy to see how Dennis' condition might symbolize for you the spirit of the times. He is not a single person, but pieces of the many he has touched. And these pieces do not fit together. They clash. Still, he is there, somewhere, just like humanity. —What is there to fight, and how do you fight it? You hold with the hope, which is not unwarranted. You do not let your fear slide over into despair. You do not withdraw. You feed your fear

33

to the hope. Burn it. Transform it into a patient expectancy.

You counsel a hard course, Lydia. . . .

I know. I know, too, that you will do it.

I will—try. . . .

A cold wind from the mountains came and rustled the geraniums. Vicki leaned back and felt it on her face, her eyes looking past the adobe wall, up to the place where the shadow-clad mountain seemed suddenly poised above them.

"He is a child of a special time," she said then. "I will learn to wait for him."

Lydia studied her profile, nodded finally, rose.

"I wish to be with him again for a time," she said.

"Yes. Go."

Vicki sat until night with its stars came above her. At length, she realized it was cold and withdrew.

Autumn, winter, spring . . .
Summer.

The evening before, I had had a drink in the bar of La Fonda, the old hotel at the end of the Santa Fe Trail. Now, I regarded the front of the building and waited. Hot up here, atop the row of buildings across San Francisco. I looked past the low screening wall and up the street to my right. All the buildings were low. Very few things in this town over three stories. La Fonda itself is an exception. Adobe, stucco. Varying shades of brown, set off here and there with brick and tile. No problem, getting to this spot before daybreak, coming across rooftops as I had. But now, the sun . . . God! It blazed down on the plaza, on my back. Should have worn a long-sleeved shirt. Then I would only be roasting now. This way, I would shortly be a sunburnt corpse or a living lobster. Depending on how things went . . . Life is more a process of what happens to you while you are waiting for things than it is the collection of things themselves.

The weapon lay at my feet, a .30/06. It was covered by the dark jacket I had worn last night. I had spent a day with it up in the hills, and even slept with it for several nights running. Yesterday, I had stripped it down, cleaned it, oiled it. Now it was loaded, ready. No need to touch it again until it was time to use it. Another might pick it up, fondle it, fool with it, replace it, return to it. Since the bulk of life is waiting, my feelings have always been that one should learn to do it well. The world comes at you through the senses. There is no way to prevent this wholly, short of death, nor should I desire to. It forces a model of itself upon your inner being. So, willing or not, I have it inside me here. Its will is therefore stronger than my own, and I am part of everything it has shown me. Truly, the highest form of activity in which I might engage is its contemplation. But who can be continuously comfortable with ultimates? I would not have minded smoking as I waited, a thing I did in earlier days before I saw how things worked. The other Children of the Earth would say that it is bad for the health and an incidental air pollutant. For me, the air pollution is enough. Too much, actually. Though the world is greater than I am, I know that it can be hurt. I wish to refrain from doing so in as many areas as possible. Even if the results are negligible, I would see them entered into the image of the world within me with an awareness of myself as their agent. This would disturb me at times of waiting and contemplation; that is to say, much of the time. As to its effects on my health, this would trouble me not at all. I do not much care what becomes of me. A man is born, lives, dies. Given infinity, I will be dead as long as anyone else. Unless there is something to reincarnation, as some of them say ... In that case, though, it does not matter either. All that does matter is to build the image and enjoy it, to keep from disturbing its balances, to refrain from harming it. ... Or, as I am going to do now, some positive thing to improve it or protect it. That is virtue, the only virtue I can see. If I die bearing with me a better image than would have existed but for my efforts, then I will have passed fulfilled, having rendered the Earth my mother some payment for my keep, some token of gratitude for the time of my existence. As for what becomes of me in the process, let them write: Roderick Leishman. He didn't much care what became of him.

Two State cars purred up the street and hissed to a halt before the entrance of La Fonda. I leaned forward as a State trooper emerged from the building and went to speak with the drivers. Soon, soon now . . . I'd helped blow two dams during the past year. That makes six for the COE, and two nuclear power plants. The Children have been busy. Today, though, we might accomplish a lot more. Stop the damage before it begins. Wheeler and McCormack, governors of Wyoming and Colorado, here to meet with the governor of New Mexico to discuss large-scale energy projects— large-scale exploitation, pollution, corruption, destruction. I bear them no personal malice, though. Shouldn't have read as much about them as I did. Not all that bad, as individuals. But the Earth is more important. Their deaths will mean more than *their* deaths. . . .

I watched the trooper turn and head back into La Fonda. Slowly—no real hurry necessary—I leaned and uncovered my weapon. I raised it then and held it across my knees. I had already chalked the sign of the Children of the Earth on the wall beside me.

Not too much longer now, I'd say. . . .

Two troopers emerged and held the doors, one of them the man who had been out to speak with the chauffeurs. They did not even look up and down the street. I shifted my weapon, pulled the stock back up to my shoulder, curled my finger about the trigger.

Four men passed out through the doors, talking among themselves. I had no trouble with identification, at this distance. My first shot, a clean and easy one, dropped Wheeler. I twitched the barrel to the side and hit McCormack twice, as I was not sure where my first one took him. Then I lowered myself, wiped the weapon quickly but carefully as planned, leaned it against the wall, turned, crouching, and began my retreat along the rooftops. I heard shots at my back, but nothing came close.

Now, if only *my* chauffeur was in the proper place, I

could begin the car-switching routine that would get me out and away. . . . While I do not much care what becomes of me, I make the effort to prolong the waiting, Mother Earth, that I might serve you as you deserve. I—

Summer.

Vicki dropped her trowel at the mental equivalent of a shriek.

Lydia—? she began, but by then she was aware of the cause.

She left the greenhouse, ran through the courtyard, entered the house.

Partway across the living room, she felt Lydia's thoughts, soothing, surprisingly controlled: *It is all right. You have not been hurt. You must not get excited.*

Then, the voice she had never heard before: "My shoulder— I think it's broken! I have to get down!"

She rushed forward, pushed past Lydia.

Dennis had gotten off the bed. He was standing at its side, leaning against it. He clutched his right shoulder with his left hand and cast his eyes wildly about the room.

"There!" he cried, and then he stumbled forward and fell.

She hurried to him.

"Victoria! Get out of here!" Lydia called.

She raised him in her arms.

"He's hurt," Vicki replied.

"He is not hurt. Children fall all the time. I will have to ask you to leave."

"But he's never gotten out before—or talked. I have to—"

"Leave! I mean it! Give him to me and get out! I know what I am doing!"

Vicki kissed him and surrendered the shaking boy.

". . . And stay out of his mind, too. That is very important. I cannot be responsible if you intervene at crucial times."

"All right. I'm going. Come tell me about it as soon as you can."

She rose and departed.

As she crossed the living room, Dennis began to shout again. She looked at all the chairs, then realized she did not want to sit down. She moved to the kitchen and set some water to boil.

Later—she did not know how much later—she found herself seated at the breakfast bar, staring into a cup of tea. When Lydia came in and took a cup, she waited for the other to speak.

Lydia shook her head and sat down beside her.

"I do not know," she said, "exactly what happened. It was more than a hallucination. He had hold of a genuine personality structure—an adult one. Since he lacks one of his own to override it, it occupied him completely. I was able to stimulate his sleep centers and he is now resting. When he awakens, this may have vanished entirely."

"Do you think I should call Dr. Winchell?"

"No, this is in no way out of line with the diagnosis. It is simply more spectacular than the early effects. Basically, Dennis has no personality, no self, of his own. He is a traumatized collection of fragments of other people whose minds he encountered before you moved here. Somehow, he has encountered another and the same thing has occurred, on a larger scale. The individual was undergoing some stressful experience, and Dennis—who is more developed neurologically now—seized hold of a larger chunk of that person's psyche. As to who and where, I did not take the time to probe at length. If there is a recurrence, I will have to. In the meantime, it may even work to Dennis' benefit. I may be able to utilize some of the new material in the structuring of his own personality. It is too early to say, of course, but it is a possibility."

"Then he was not hurt?"

"No. The person with whom he was in contact had been hurt. He was reacting to that."

"I had better call Dick and let him know what has happened."

"You may be disturbing him unduly. I think it would be better to wait and see what the situation is tomorrow. You would have a more complete story to tell him then."

"That is true. He is gone so much of the time now, Lydia. . . . Do you think he is running away from—this?"

"Perhaps to some extent. But the nature of his work—the new union negotiations . . . You know that this is a bona fide business trip. The feeling that he is running away may be a projection of your own desires. It has been a while since you have been away, has it not?"

"God! Yes!"

"Perhaps when this small crisis is past you ought to consider taking a vacation. I could manage things here in your absence."

"You may be right. I will think about it, Lydia. Thanks."

When Vicki rose, late the following morning, Lydia was already in Dennis' room. It was a warm, sunny day, and she worked in the greenhouse till lunchtime. When Lydia did not join her as usual she approached the closed door and stood there a long while before returning to the kitchen. Gentle feelers of thought had detected intense mental activity within. She pressed the general button on the news unit, cut out the viewer, pressed for a repro copy. One by one, sheets slid into the tray. She stopped it at two dozen, gathered the stack, took it with her to the table.

Later, she went to sit in the courtyard, and after a time she slept.

For long moments, she did not know whether she had been dreaming. . . .

She lay there, blinking up at the light. The shadows had lengthened. Somewhere a jay was calling.

Then, *Victoria, where are you?*

She sat up.

What is it?

The news . . . Dennis' fixe *. . . The story is right*

here! Governor Wheeler dead, and McCormack seriously injured . . . "Assassin fled . . . believed wounded . . ." Dennis was in that man's mind, was still there today. I could not sever the connection. I finally put him to sleep again. I thought he had contacted someone who was fantasizing vividly—a psychotic, perhaps— but I was wrong. This is real—and it was in Santa Fe.

Santa Fe is over a hundred miles from here!

I know! Dennis' ability has apparently increased. Or else Dr. Winchell's tests were faulty.

I had better call the doctor—and Dick.

We had better call the authorities, too. I know the man's name—Roderick Leishman. He is a member of that radical eco group, the Children of the Earth. I had the impression he was heading north.

I am coming. Will you make the calls? Except to Dick.

Of course.

We made it to a COE farm in Colorado that evening. I had lain in the rear of vehicle after vehicle— four, to be exact—clutching my shoulder much of the time. The second driver had gotten some gauze and tape and bandaged it. He had also gotten me aspirins and a fifth of bourbon. These helped quite a bit.

Jerry's and Betty's place is sort of a communal farm. Everyone on it is COE, but only Jerry and Betty and a guy called Quick Smith knew what I had been about and knew that I might show up in need of help. The fewer in on it the better, like always. They took me right to a bedroom they had had ready in the main building, where Jerry dug out the .38 long under a local, cleaned the wound and sewed it up, ground some bones together, plastered me up, shot me full of antibiotics and fitted me with a sling. He was a veterinarian. We did not have a reliable M.D. in the area.

"How many of those damn aspirins did you take?" he asked me.

"Maybe a dozen. Maybe more."

Jerry was a tall, gaunt man, who could have been anywhere between thirty and fifty. He had sweated away everything but sinews and calluses, leaving behind a lot of facial creases. He wore steel-rimmed spectacles, and his lips grew thinner whenever he was angry.

"Don't you know what they do to the clotting factor?"

"No."

"They screw it up. You bleed more. You lost a lot of blood. You should probably have a transfusion."

"I'll live," I said. "I made it this far without going into shock."

He nodded and his glasses flashed.

"Give me a horse any time," he said. "Booze and aspirin. And nothing to eat all day."

I started a shrug, reconsidered immediately.

"I'd have chosen a better menu under other circumstances—and if I were a horse, you might have shot me."

He chuckled, then sobered.

"You did pull it off, though. I wasn't sure you'd make it away afterward."

"We figured it pretty carefully."

He nodded.

"How do you feel about it—now?"

"It had to be done."

"I guess so."

"You see any alternatives? We've got to try and stop them. We're making ourselves felt. They will be treading a lot more carefully after today."

"I see it," he said. "It is just that I wish there was another way. I am still something of a lay preacher, you know? But it is not just that. It is mainly that I don't like to see things killed or hurt. One of the reasons I'm a vet. It's my feeling, not my thinking, that goes against it."

"I know," I told him. "Don't you think I thought about it for a long time? Maybe too much, even."

"I guess so. I think you ought to reconsider moving on, and spend the night here. You need the rest."

I shook my head.

"I know I do. I wish I could. I have to keep moving, though. I am still too close to where it happened to

41

rest easy. Besides, the new vehicle is a van. It has a mattress in the back. I can stretch out there. Anyway, it's better for you if I move along as quickly as possible."

"If I was worried about my own safety, I would never have gotten involved in the first place. No. That's not it. It goes back to my feeling about not liking to see things hurt or dead."

"Well, I stand a better chance of avoiding both if I cloud the trail as much as I can."

He moved to the window, looked out.

"That may be your ride coming along the road now. What color is it?"

"Red."

"Yep. It could be. Listen, I don't want you taking any more aspirins."

"Okay. I'll stick with the booze."

"Polluting your system."

"Better than polluting the Earth," I said. "It's going to be around a lot longer. Care to join me?"

He gave a brief chuckle, followed by a skeletal grin.

"One for the road? Well, why not?"

I fetched my bottle while he got a pair of glasses from the cupboard. I let him pour.

"Safe journey," he said.

"Thanks. Good harvest."

I heard the van draw up. I crossed to the window and looked out. Quick Smith, lithe and prematurely white-haired, who, but for the flip of a coin, would have been in my place, moved to check it out. I recognized the driver, though. So I finished my drink without haste, returned the glass to the counter, retrieved my bottle.

I clasped Jerry's hand.

"Go light on that stuff just the same, hear?"

I nodded vaguely, just as Quick came in to announce the arrival.

"So long."

I followed him outside, got into the back of the thing. The driver, a beefy lad named Fred, came around to see how I was and to show me where things were. There was food, a water jug, a bottle of wine, a .38 revolver and a box of cartridges. I wasn't sure what use the last might prove—if someone caught up with me, I would go willingly enough—and I was not in a position to load it too quickly anyhow. Seeing this, Fred loaded it for me and stashed it under the mattress.

"Ready?" he said.

I nodded and he locked me in. I lay down and closed my eyes.

Dr. Winchell had been unable to persuade Lieutenant Martinez, but during a ten-minute phone call he had been able to convince Richard Guise. Dick had required only a five-minute call across Washington to arouse federal interest to the extent that Special Agent Robertson was at the Guise home that evening. Robertson, thirty, clean, kempt, blue-eyed, gray-garbed and unsmiling, came to sit in the living room across from Vicki and Lydia.

"There is no file on anyone named Roderick Leishman," he said.

"I cannot help that," Lydia told him. "That is his name."

Vicki looked in her direction, surprised by the tone of her voice. Lydia's chin was somewhat raised, her mouth tight.

"Sorry," Robertson said. "No offense. They are still checking. He might have used a different name in the past. You were right about the COE connection. He did leave their sign."

She nodded.

"Tell me," she said. "What will become of him?"

Robertson began a smile, suppressed it.

"The usual. Trial, conviction, sentencing—if your information is correct. As to the details, they will depend on his attorney, the jury, the judge. You know."

"That was not what I meant," she said.

He cocked his head.

"I am afraid I do not understand."

"I was thinking of my patient," she said. "His tele-

43

pathic fixation on the fugitive amounts to total absorption. I want some sort of assurance that if we assist you the man will be brought in alive. I have no idea what effect his death would have on Dennis. I do not wish to find out."

"I cannot give you any assurance—"

"Then I may not be able to give you any assistance."

"Withholding evidence is a serious matter. Especially in a case like this."

"My first duty, as I see it, is to my patient. For that matter, though, I am not even certain this comes under the heading of evidence. I do not believe there has ever been a case involving anything of this sort."

Robertson sighed.

"Let's not quibble over the legalities," he said. "The man has shot two governors. One is dead and the other may not make it through the night. He is a member of a radical eco group which includes violence as part of its program. He is running around loose now and you admit Dennis can follow him. If you refuse to cooperate, we can bring in a telepath of our own to monitor Dennis. You are not at all that necess—"

"Mr. Robertson, there are very clear legal precedents in that area. You would be invading his privacy in the highest sense—"

"He is a minor. Parental consent is all that is required, and you are not his parent."

He looked at Vicki, who clasped her hands very tightly and turned toward Lydia.

"Dennis would be hurt if they hurt the man?" she said.

"I think so."

"Then I do *not* give my consent," she said. "I am sorry, Mr. Robertson."

"Inasmuch as your husband started this, it is possible that he will give us the release."

Vicki's hands suddenly relaxed.

"If he does," she said, "I will never speak to him again. I will leave and take Dennis with me."

Robertson bowed his head.

44

"I am not trying to be unreasonable," he said. "Can you tell me how I could possibly guarantee what you are asking? We want him alive. We want to question him. We want to learn as much about his group as we can. We are going to try to take him alive. But men will shoot in self-defense. Even then, they would try not to kill him. But it is possible. He could be killed. *You* try to be reasonable. If you give us exact information concerning him, it will up our chances of landing him whole. What else can I offer you?"

"Very well," said Lydia. "You make some sense. What you can do then is communicate all this to whatever field agents get involved in the pursuit."

"Done," he said. "I will personally talk with them at whatever office gets involved. You can listen to what I say. Fair enough?"

Lydia looked at Vicki.

Go ahead, Vicki indicated.

"All right," Lydia began. "He is in Colorado. . . ."

It was still dark when I awoke. I was very thirsty, and my shoulder was throbbing. It took me several moments to recall what had happened. I leaned forward then and located the water bottle. I rubbed my eyes, ran my hands through my hair, took another drink.

I pushed the curtain aside and looked out the window. Rocks, fenceposts, sandy soil . . .

I checked my watch: 4:35.

"Would you pull over somewhere?" I called out. "My bladder's busting."

He stopped and let me out. I went over to the ditch.

"How much longer till the next switchpoint?" I asked him.

"Half an hour. Maybe less. We're supposed to meet around five."

I grunted.

"How are you holding up?" he asked.

"I'll be okay," I said. "Any trouble while I was sleeping?"

"No trouble. Nothing new on the news either."

45

I climbed back inside.

It was chilly, so I sat with the blanket around my shoulders. I took a drink of the bourbon. It would seem that we had to be free of pursuit after all this time. I ran my hand over my chin. I would stop shaving, I decided, grow a beard. Let my hair get longer, too. Lay up till the shoulder was better, then get some simple job. Stay at it three, four months . . . Drift west. Seattle, Portland . . .

I felt the bump in the mattress. Did I want to take the pistol with me? Trouble to be found with it. Good to have, though. I considered concealing it in the sling. Good place for it. Probably ought to keep it till I recovered. Ditch it then. Wish they had picked a smaller piece, though.

I withdrew the weapon, tried it in different positions in the sling. It was least apparent toward the back. Snug enough. Easy to reach. Almost a shame to pass up such a neat means of concealment.

I removed it and returned it to the place beneath the mattress. Something to think about, anyway . . .

Still chilled. I took a long pull at the bottle. Better, that. Better than aspirin. No reason not to be a little high.

After a time, we slowed, turned off the road and ground along a rocky surface. Moments later, we halted and he came around and opened the back.

"Okay, we're here," he told me.

"Where's here?"

"McKinley, Wyoming."

I whistled.

"We've come a good distance."

He gave me his hand, helped me down. Then he climbed inside. He gathered the blanket, the pillow, the water bottle, the fifth, placing them within easy reach on the floor behind him. He groped beneath the mattress and drew out the pistol. He glanced at me, glanced at the weapon, then back at me.

"You taking this, too?"

"Why not?" I said, and I accepted the piece and thrust it into my sling.

A glister of sleekshifting starlight, low, to my right . . .

"What lake is that?"

"Glendo Reservoir."

He stepped down, turned, picked up the stuff.

He rounded the van and I followed him, becoming aware of a parked vehicle beneath some trees, perhaps a hundred feet away. The damp air was still, the night empty of sound except for that of our own progress. As we neared, I saw that it was a long green sedan. The driver sat smoking, watching us approach. I greeted him, did not recognize him. No names were exchanged.

My driver nodded to him, loaded my things into the back, clasped my good shoulder.

"Good luck," he said.

"Thanks."

I got in, made myself comfortable.

"How are you holding up?" said the new driver.

"Pretty well. Considering."

I heard the engine chuckle and whisper. An arc, a spatter of fire as the driver disposed of his weed. The headlights came on. We moved forward.

A little later the driver said, "It's in all the news. What was it like?"

"It's mostly waiting," I said. "Doing it just takes a few seconds. A mechanical action. Then you are thinking about getting away."

Those few seconds went through my mind again. I saw them fall. I had already made the mark. I wiped the weapon and leaned it . . . so. Then I was crouched, running. I heard the noises behind me, below. The shot . . . my shoulder . . . I had left blood. They had probably typed it by now.

"Nothing special," I said. "It's all over."

"McCormack is still hanging on, last I heard."

"It doesn't matter. The gesture is enough. Hope he makes it."

"*Him?*"

"A lot of people have learned something. That's enough. I want to stop thinking about it now."

47

"You think it will really do some good?"

"Who can say? I hope so. I tried."

"It might take a few more incidents like this to really get the point across."

"Incidents, hell! It was a killing. Someone else can do the next one, if it's got to be. I'm retired."

"You deserve a rest."

My shoulder was throbbing again. I opened the bottle.

"Want a drink?"

"Yeah, thanks."

He took it, took a slug, passed it back.

I thought of the waiting, of the image of the Earth in my mind and how I hoped I had changed it. . . . I looked out the window at the shadow shapes of rock and scrub, plain and hill. I wished for a little rain, to rinse things over, for some wind, to blow them dry and clean. But the land lay still and rugged. So be it. I may dislike it this way, yet it pleases me also that the grasses are dry and the animals in their burrows. The pleasure and the pride of humanity are best enjoyed against the heedlessness, the slumbering power of the Earth. Even when it moves to crush, it adds something. To isolate oneself too much from it detracts from both our achievements and our failures. We must feel the forces we live with. . . .

I opened the window and breathed deeply.

Yes. The world was still breathing life into my lungs, and I was grateful to give it back. . . .

"I really do not like keeping him awake this long," Lydia said, staring down at her empty coffee cup.

Robertson clamped his jaws, loosened them.

"I don't think it will be too much longer," he said, "now that the office in Casper has been alerted. He may make it out of Wyoming before they reach him, though. But with the Rapid City people heading out, too, a flier should reach him before he is too far into South Dakota. A green vehicle heading east at this hour . . . Shouldn't be too hard to spot. Another half-hour, I'd say."

Lydia glanced over at Vicki, asleep on the sofa.

"Care for some more coffee?" she asked Robertson.

"All right."

As she poured, he asked her, "Dennis' condition . . . Isn't it rather unusual for a telepath to be able to operate at this distance? Leishman is well over five hundred miles from here."

"Yes, it is," Lydia said.

"How does he do it?"

She smiled.

"We are not even certain why it works at *any* distance," she said. "But you are correct about the range. It is unprecedented to sustain contact for this long at this distance."

Robertson drained his cup.

"Then Dennis has never gone out this far before—even for short periods?"

"No. Frankly, I had thought we would just be giving you a lead, and that Dennis would have lost contact long before this."

"It must be hard on the kid. I *am* sorry."

"Actually, I feel no signs of strain in him, other than normal fatigue at being up this late past his bedtime. You know that is not my main concern—"

"I know, I know. I don't want to damage the kid's mind either. Listen, I've been thinking. Since Dennis is in such good contact, couldn't he transmit as well as receive? Try to talk Leishman into giving himself up?"

"No. Dennis would not know how to go about it."

"What about you, then? Could you operate through Dennis, get a message to Leishman that way? Tell him to stop and wait, to hand over that gun?"

"I do not know," she said. "I have never tried anything like that."

"Will you?"

She took a sip of coffee, then leaned back and closed her eyes.

"I will tell you in a few moments whether it can be done."

I placed the empty bottle on the floor, rearranged

49

the blanket for the dozenth time. Beyond the window, the world swam pleasantly. Perhaps I would sleep now. . . .

A misty, gray, humming thing of indefinite duration . . .

Roderick Leishman.

I shuddered, I rubbed my eyes and looked about. Nothing had changed.

Roderick Leishman.

"What?"

"I didn't say anything," said the driver.

"I thought someone did."

"You were asleep. Must have been dreaming."

"Must have."

I sighed and settled back again.

No, you were not dreaming, Roderick. I addressed you.

. . . The Earth Mother is aloof, heedless. She speaks to no man. I felt the bottle against my foot and chuckled. I had never heard voices before. I did not feel that drunk, but then the participant is seldom the best judge. When I awoke it would seem a dream. I closed my eyes.

. . . *Neither drunk nor dreaming, Roderick. I am with you now.*

"Who are you?" I whispered.

You have named me.

"What I did today could not have been that important."

There are other considerations.

"What is it that you want?"

Your life.

"Take it. It is yours."

I wish to preserve it, not take it.

"What do you mean?"

At this moment, you are being pursued by federal agents. They are aware of your location. They will reach you before too long.

I drew my slung arm tight, feeling the pistol against my ribs.

No. You must surrender, not fight.

"I might be worth more as a martyr."

A trial would be much better. Your motive would be detailed at great length.

"What do you want me to do now?"

Park the car and wait. Surrender yourself. Do not give your pursuers an excuse to harm you.

"I see. Will you stay with me—through it all?"

I am always with you.

I pushed back the blanket, let it fall. I leaned forward.

"Pull over for a minute, will you?" I said.

"Sure."

He braked and turned off the road. When we were halted, I said, "Do you have a gun?"

"Yes. In the glove compartment."

"Get it out."

"What's the matter?"

"Just do it, damn it!"

"Okay! Okay!"

He leaned over, opened the compartment, reached inside.

When he began to swing it in my direction, I was ready. Mine was pointed.

"Not that way," I said. "Put it down on the seat."

"What is this?"

"Do it!"

He hesitated a moment too long, and, "I've already shot two men today," I said.

He put it down.

"Now reach over with your left hand and pick it up by the barrel."

He did this.

"Pass it over. Drop it on the floor back here."

"What's going on?" he asked.

"I am trying to keep us from getting killed. Do you mind?"

"I'm all for it," he said. "I think it's a great idea. But I don't understand how disarming me will do it."

"I want to avoid a shootout. I think we are about to be arrested."

He chuckled. He opened his door.

"Don't get out!"

"I'm not." He gestured outward. "Look, though. We're all alone. No one coming, either way. Listen, I know you're very tired, you've had a lot to drink and your nerves have to be shot after everything that's happened. I understand. With all due respect, I think you're a bit delirious. Why don't you—"

"Don't move! Both hands on the wheel!"

"Look, we are going to seem suspicious if anyone comes by and sees us this way."

"Better than the alternative."

"Getting away?"

"Getting dead. We can't get away."

"Mind if I ask what makes you think so?"

"You do not have to know," I said.

He was silent for a long while. Then, "Is this some sort of setup?" he said. "A part of the plan I'm not in on? Or is it just your own idea?"

"It is not just my own idea."

He sighed.

"Oh. Why didn't you tell me sooner? I would have gone along with it, so long as you know what you're doing."

"Better you don't know."

"You can put the gun away. I—"

"I'm tired of talking. Just sit there."

Richard Guise approached his son, who rested on the courtyard bench.

"How do you do," he said.

"Hello."

"My name's Dick Guise."

Dennis rose, extended his left hand upward, turning the palm out. He held his right across his chest. His dark eyes met his father's.

"Rod Leishman," he said, as Dick clasped it and released it.

"Mind if I sit down?"

"Sit," Dennis said, seating himself.

"How are you—feeling?"

"Shoulder's still giving me some trouble." He reached across and rubbed it. "You a lawyer?"

"Friend of the court," Dick said, seating himself. "They treating you all right?"

"Can't complain. Listen, I am not sure I should be talking with you without Mr. Palmer—my regular attorney—around. Just my ignorance. Nothing personal. Okay?"

"Sure. May I ask you something not connected with the case?'

The green eyes, like Vicki's, fixed him once again.

"Go ahead."

"What do the Children of the Earth really hope to accomplish with all their violence?"

"Our only desire is to preserve the Earth and maintain it as a suitable habitation for mankind."

"By killing people? By blowing up power plants and dams?"

"It seems the only way to convince those in authority that we are serious."

"Let me put it this way. If you were actually to succeed in removing the large sources of energy, you would probably defeat your own aim of maintaining the Earth as a suitable habitation for mankind. Wait! Let me finish. I do not know whether you have ever read Robert Heilbroner's *The Future as History,* written back in the middle of the last century, but he makes a good case for the premise that the major outlines of the future were already history in that they followed ineluctably from the forces already in operation, that they were so powerful we could barely oppose the general course they were determining for us. Technology, for example, would have to advance. This, in turn, would lead to an increasingly bureaucratic state. Abundant production would make living sufficiently easy that economic pressure would not, in itself, be enough to keep people in the less attractive occupations. He proved right on these matters, and on the lesser developed countries springing for whatever political system promised the most rapid industrialization. From there, their futures will follow as ours did—"

"Heilbroner was a shrewd man," Dennis said, "but you cannot project a curve like that forever. The system breaks down before—"

"Technology is proving capable of finding answers to the problems it has created."

"But not enough and not fast enough. The world keeps growing, complicating, overproducing the wrong things. The standard of living is too high when people exist for the sake of industry instead of the other way around. Thoreau—"

"Thoreau and Rousseau and that whole crowd would like to see us all living in the woods again."

"Rousseau has generally been misunderstood, and Thoreau never said that. What they were all getting at, I think, was something like a science of the optimum, an understanding of just how large, how complex, how mechanized, how populous a society should be so as to provide the best life for its people—a science to determine these things and a will to be guided by them. They did not want to go back to the woods, but to find the most suitable middle ground between the basic and the complex. That is what the Children really want."

Dick was silent a moment, then said, "That sounds very noble, and it seems that you are sincere. I am certainly not against idealism. We need ideals. But I feel Heilbroner was correct. We write the history of the future a long time in advance. I hope, and believe, that it will go your way one day. But we have to lose a lot of momentum first, rechannel a lot of energies. Something like that takes generations. It cannot be accomplished overnight. Least of all, it cannot be accomplished by random acts of violence against what has already been built up."

"We haven't got that kind of time," Dennis said. "And I believe Heilbroner can be made wrong about the way we write the history of the future, if we are sufficiently determined to learn from the errors of the past."

"And if we do not, I still do not see chaos waiting around the next corner."

"Then I hope yours is the right corner, but I doubt it."

Dick rose.

"I have to go inside now. I'll see you around."

Dennis nodded.

"Be seeing you."

He hurried away from the small form on the bench without looking back. Entering the house, he passed through the living room without speaking to Vicki and Lydia, who were seated on the sofa. In the kitchen, he poured himself a stiff drink, downed it, poured another, turned, walked slowly back to the front room.

"I still do not believe it," he said, lowering himself into an armchair. "A few weeks ago he was a vegetable. Now ... Lydia, you told me he was in contact with the guy, not that he had assumed his entire personality."

"This is a new development," Lydia explained. "It occurred after we spoke with you, before you returned."

"He is not even acting out the man's predicament. He is responding to new stimuli as if he *were* Leishman."

"Yes."

"How long is this going to last?"

"There is no way of telling."

"Is it a good sign or a bad one?"

"Good, I would say. No matter what happens now, there should be some residue, some remnant of the synaptic processes that have been taking place."

"But is he going to grow up thinking he *is* Leishman?"

"Not if we intervene—which we will, if the effect continues too long. The important thing now is that there is something there, some activity within his skull. His brain needs the workout it is getting. It has been idle too long."

"But those aren't kid thoughts going through it. They are adult thoughts. Mightn't the premature exposure warp him for whatever is to come later?"

Vicki chuckled, and Dick seemed to notice her for the first time.

"You seem to be forgetting that a bombardment of adult thoughts is what caused his problem in the first place. Now, at least, he has learned to filter them and focus on one mind at a time. So what if he is doing it exclusively with Leishman? I have spoken with him at length since this occurred. This Leishman is not all that bad a chap. In fact, I rather like him. He is an idealist and—"

"—a murderer," Dick finished. "Yeah, a great guy our son picked. Lydia, is this going to hurt him later on?"

"Did it hurt you?" she asked. "Or you, Victoria? You were both exposed to adult thoughts at an early age. Were either of you permanently damaged by the experience?"

" 'Exposed,' not totally absorbed," Dick said. "There is a big difference."

Lydia nodded.

"All right," she said. "Of course there is the possibility of long-term influence. I am convinced, however, that therapy can correct it if it does occur. But I would rather wait until there is more to work with before I tackle the problem of identity."

"How dependent is Dennis on Leishman? I mean, supposing the man were to drop dead right now? What would happen to Dennis? Would he go on thinking he is Leishman, or would he fall apart again?"

"That is one of those questions which simply cannot be answered from the facts that we have. There *is* still a connection. He is apparently aware of everything that happens to the man. Yet he also acts independently in terms of the other's identity. I do not know where the line is drawn."

"I think we had better find out. You will need to know that when it comes time to straighten him out."

"I will deal with the problem when it comes due."

"Something suggests itself," Dick said. "What is Dennis' range, anyway? He is keeping tabs on Leishman at over a hundred miles, now that he has been returned, but he followed him for over five hundred miles. What might his upper limit be?"

Lydia shook her head.

"Again, not enough data."

"Exactly," Dick said. "I would like to find out, though. Once he has his mind in shape and has reached maturity, he might well be the greatest telepath the race has yet produced."

"He probably is," Vicki said. "That is what caused his problem."

"Supposing I take him to Europe with me next month? He will have had plenty of time to play with his new synapses. We will pull him out of range of Leishman and see whether he is still dependent on the guy or whether he has absorbed enough to keep functioning as he is."

"I would advise against it," Lydia said. "Supposing he simply retreats into catatonia?"

"Then we bring him back and let him be Leishman again for a while."

"But we do not know that he would pick up on Leishman again. He might simply remain withdrawn."

"Then your theory is wrong, and the sooner we know it the better."

"I can see you have already decided."

"Yes. Even given the worst, the situation would simply revert to one you have already assured us holds hope. What is the difference, really?"

Lydia lowered her head.

"I cannot honestly say."

Dick finished his drink.

"So there," he said. "We'll do it."

"Very well. But either I accompany him—with the understanding that I bring him home immediately if there are any problems—or I leave the case."

"Lydia, you can't!" Vicki said.

"It is the only way."

"All right," Dick said, "I agree. It is something I have to find out, though."

"Lydia," Vicki said. "Could this really hurt Dennis' chances?"

"I think so."

"Then I forbid it. Dick, you are not going to ruin

what is left of my son just to determine his TP range. If you insist on this, I'm leaving. I will get a court order if necessary to prevent your moving him."

Dick reddened.

"Vicki. I—"

"You heard me. What will it be?"

"I think you are being silly."

"I do not really care what you think. What are you going to do?"

"You give me no choice. I won't take him. I thought it was a good idea. I still do. Lydia, what about next spring? I am going over again then. Would that be more propitious?"

"Possibly. Probably, even. There would have been more time for him to adjust to functioning."

"Okay, let's talk about it again then. Vicki, I am sorry. I did not realize . . ."

"I know. But now you do."

"Now I do."

Dick took his glass back to the kitchen and rinsed it.

"I think I am going to change and take a walk," he called out.

Vicki rose, headed for the courtyard.

Lydia crossed the room and stared out the window, fingering her pendant as she watched the mountains and the clouds.

Dick was in the East that autumn, when Roderick Leishman's case was heard. Therefore, it was from Winchell's calls following his weekly examinations of Dennis that he learned of the boy's alternate elation and depression as the trial progressed. The news media were unaware of Dennis' connection with the case, and only two other medical consultants knew of his condition.

Dick regarded Winchell in the viewer.

"He still bathes himself and dresses himself . . . ?" Dick said.

"Yes."

"He still feeds himself, and he responds intelligently when people talk to him?"

"In the character of Leishman . . . yes."

"He still seems aware of everything that Leishman thinks or does?"

"We have checked periodically on the factual aspect of it, and this does seem to be the case."

"I find it difficult to understand how he manages to respond to two separate environments and not grow confused, not become aware of the contradictions in the situation."

"Well, it is similar to the classic paranoid reaction where the patient can function relatively well in his normal environment yet still believe he is someone else, somewhere else."

"I think I see, sort of. How long do you figure this will go on?"

"No way of telling yet, as I've said before. But I agree with Lydia that it is a situation worth exploiting. Let it sink in. She can take care of personality tailoring later."

"What about the trip I mentioned?"

"The way that I see it is that if he really is going to benefit from this exposure, he should have had enough of it by spring. I don't see why the cord can't be cut at that time, and let the adjustment begin."

"Good," Dick said. "About Lydia . . ."

"Yes?"

"I was just wondering. With all these new developments, is she still the best therapist for Dennis?"

"Is there something about her you don't like?"

"No, not that. I just wanted to be sure Dennis had the best."

"He does. Lydia knows Dennis better than anyone else. It would take months for another therapist to catch up on something like this—and then there is the matter of her rapport with him. It could prove disastrous to pull her off the case and bring in someone else at this point."

"I see. Just wanted to be sure."

"Is something bothering you—about her?"

"Not at all. How do you feel the verdict on the Leishman case will affect him? The man is bound to be convicted."

"Some depression, most likely. Still, Leishman seems something of a stoic, according to the psychiatrists who examined him. Dennis will simply take it the same way he does."

"It shouldn't be too far off."

"No. This week, I'd guess."

"Well, keep me posted."

"I will."

Dick decided to take his secretary to lunch and think about other things. And he was not surprised some time later when Leishman was found guilty. It was the sentencing that troubled him.

"I did not think they would take the psychiatric angle that seriously," he said to Winchell as soon as he heard of it.

"I did. There was always a possibility of this. Basically, it was his attorney's doing. I would not take it all that seriously."

"Well, they have him up at the State Hospital in Las Vegas, so he is still too close to Dennis—and now, if they start giving him therapy ... What will happen if they put him on drugs or fool with his brain? I don't like it."

Winchell was silent for a time. Then, "I see the point. I had wanted to keep Dennis—and us—out of the whole thing. Now, though, we had better find a way of keeping posted as to what course of treatment they plan for Leishman. Perhaps we can still keep it quiet. I will see whether I can work out something with the hospital. If not, we may have to go through the court."

"Well, we had better do something, quickly. The kid is screwed up enough as it is."

"Right. I will call them now and let you know."

"I still think we ought to move out of range and let it go at that."

Winchell gnawed his lip.

"Let's save that for last," he said.

I thought I had caught glimpses of him earlier in the day, but I was not certain until late afternoon, when he came by the reading room where I sat alone, turning pages. He parked the cart he had been pushing, blocking the doorway with it, stepped in, gave a low whistle and winked when I looked up.

"Quick!" I said. "What—?"

He raised a finger to his lips, turned and fetched in a carton from the lower shelf of the carryall. He brought it over and placed it on the opposite side of my chair, out of sight from the hall.

"No problem," he whispered. "I've worked in these places before. My record is clean. Got in here almost two weeks ago. How have they been treating you?"

"Observation and tests all month," I said. "What are you up to?"

He stroked the side of his sharp nose and smiled a yellow smile.

"We're getting you out of here, now. It's all set up. I have the schedule down pat. The car is waiting."

"It's still daylight. Wouldn't it be better if—"

"No. Trust me. I know where everyone is."

I regarded his slight figure, his dark, dancing eyes, pale hair, nimble fingers.

"You're shifty enough," I said. "Okay. What do I do?"

"Get into the clothes in that bundle while I go stand outside by my cart. If anyone comes, I'll whistle and you start taking them off again fast. I will come back inside with the box and you toss them back into it. Okay?"

I nodded and began unbuttoning my shirt.

"No," he said. "Put them on over your things. It's just an orderly uniform."

He moved back to the door.

"How is the shoulder?"

"Fine now. How are Jerry and Betty?"

"Well. You never got traced to them."

He stood fooling with his cart, blocking the door.

"Hey! There's a gun in here!"

61

"Sh! Stick it in your belt, under the coat. You never can tell."

I checked it. It was loaded. I stowed it. I dressed.

"All right," I said.

"Come on out then. Help me push this cart."

I stepped into the hall, got behind the cart at his side nearest the wall. We began pushing.

"Where to?" I asked.

"Service elevator, through those doors at the end. I have the key here."

We passed along the hall. He unlocked the doors. No one in sight. He unlocked the elevator. We took the cart inside and he pressed the button for the basement.

"I'll stand in front," he said. "If anyone comes by, bend over the cart real quick."

"Right."

I listened to the hum, the occasional creaking of the elevator about us. A wave of cool air passed from the left. I felt myself in a kind of daze. It was difficult to believe things were happening this quickly, with no advance warning. Just as well, too, probably. If I had had time to think it over, I might not be moving this casually. I probably would not have slept last night.

The elevator ground to a halt. Quick drew open the gate, looked outside, nodded to me, tugged on the cart.

I followed him out, pushing. We were in a half-lit hallway, but things looked to be brighter around the corner to the left. We moved in that direction, and he gestured for me to change places with him. I got over to his left before we turned the corner, left again. There was a ramp leading up to an open area—a loading dock where two workmen sat on crates, drinking coffee and smoking. The nearer man glanced in our direction as we moved upward, wheels rattling. Quick pretty much blocked his view of me.

"Damn it!" he muttered. "They don't usually take their break right on the dock."

A white van with the words "Simpson's Foods" stenciled in red on its side was backed against the dock, rear gate lowered. The door on the driver's side was open, and a man in a green uniform sat sideways, legs dangling, checking over some papers on a clipboard, a steaming cup balanced on the dash to his right. Quick waved to him and he waved back. Moments later, he swiveled forward and slammed the door. Shortly after that, he dumped the coffee out the window.

Quick slowed.

"I was simply going to close you in back and let him drive off with you," he whispered. "No good now. Those guys would know something was up." He jerked his head toward the laborers. "I am going to have to go along now—and so are they, I'm afraid."

"Guess we don't have much choice."

He shook his head.

"We stop the cart when we're abreast of them," he said, looking out past the truck and back down the ramp. "Then we stroll over. Get your gun out then and get them aboard the truck."

"Okay."

We halted the cart when we were near, turned and moved in their direction. I grinned and rested my hand on the butt of the pistol.

"Hi," Quick said, "I was just wondering . . ."

The nearer man was squinting at me. I drew the weapon and pointed it at them.

". . . wondering whether you wanted to try and be heroes, or just live and let live."

"It's Leishman," he said to the other.

"God!" the other replied.

"What'll it be?" Quick asked.

"Whatever you want," the second man said.

"Then get in the truck, both of you."

They got to their feet. The first man raised his arms.

"Put your hands down," I said. "Don't do anything conspicuous like that again."

"Sorry."

He lowered them, they headed for the truck, got in. Quick climbed down from the dock, went forward and was talking with the driver, who kept glancing back, an unhappy look on his face.

I followed the men inside.

"All the way back," I said, "and sit on the floor."

63

I seated myself across from them. Seconds later, the engine spun and caught. There was a scrambling noise from outside, and Quick rounded the corner and climbed in.

"He'll be around to shut it in a second," he said, taking up a position to my right, legs stretched out before him.

A light came on overhead.

The man across from me on the left, a young, slight, dark-haired guy, said, "What are you going to do with us?"

"Nothing," I said, "if you don't make any trouble. You know you would report someone leaving in the truck. We can't have that. Be good, don't make any noises as we leave, and we'll drop you in the boondocks as soon as we're out a ways. Okay?"

"Anything you say," he said. "I've got a family."

"So do I," said the older man beside him. "I'll do what you say."

"Then sit back and enjoy the ride," I said.

The driver came around and Quick went back and whispered with him before he closed us in. Moments later, I heard his door slam. Then the engine started. Presently, we were moving.

Quick leaned over and whispered to me, "We are going to drop them before we switch vehicles. The less they know, the better."

"Good idea. How long will that be?"

"Around twenty minutes, I figure. We ditch them in fifteen."

"Good enough."

The situation finally reached me at an animal level, and I felt a profound desire to pace. My palms began to perspire and I wiped them on my trousers. Ridiculous. I had had no particular reactions when I had done the shooting in Santa Fe. It was probably that I had worked them all off in advance, contemplating the event. This time, however, without preparation, I was easy prey to the uncertainties involved.

We halted. Outer gate. I heard voices but could not distinguish the words. Shortly, we were moving again.

"Mind if I smoke?" the man across from me asked.

"Go ahead," I said.

I watched him light up.

"Could I have one of those?" I asked.

"Sure." He extended the pack.

I got up, crossed over and took one.

"May I have a light?"

He passed me his matches.

"Thanks," I said, handing them back.

I returned to my place across from him and reseated myself.

"That was stupid," said Quick. "You could have had one of mine."

"Didn't know you smoked."

"Haven't had a chance to," he said, producing one and lighting it. "I didn't know you smoked."

"I haven't, for years. I just decided to balance an ecological loss against a psychological gain. My chances are better if I'm relaxed. Anything I can do to improve my chances right now is worth it. If I get away, I may be able to carry off some more big ones for the Children. Ah! that's good!"

"You're a weird guy," Quick said. "I sometimes get the feeling the whole movement is more of a religious thing for you than it is anything else."

"That's fair," I said. "I guess it is."

"You think you'll get pie in the sky for whatever you do?"

"Satisfaction right here is more than enough. The Earth is my reward as well as my concern."

"They said at the trial that you used to be with the Forest Service. I never knew that."

I nodded.

"What the lawyer said was true. It does all go back to that, for me—seeing the land and everything on it constantly taking second place to commercial interests. I talked with COE people on and off for a couple years. Finally, one day, I decided hell! if we are as brutal to them as they are to the land, maybe then some of the exploiters will get the point, think twice. . . . I don't know. I had to do something besides writing protest

65

letters. I get this kind of—mystical—feeling sometimes, when I am out in the country. I feel there is something—some force—I am serving. It does not matter what it is. It does not even matter whether it is really there. I am sometimes comforted by a sense of presence that seems kindly disposed toward me. That is enough."

"You've lived out of doors a lot then?"

"Yes, I have."

Quick glanced at the guys across from us, lowered his voice:

"You could live off the land, then?"

"Yes."

"Maybe that wouldn't be a bad idea, till things cool down. Lots of places, say, in Canada where they would never find you."

"I've thought of it. —What about yourself? Why are you in the movement?"

"Nothing as fancy as your reasons. I envy them, but nothing's ever seen fit to give me the mystic high-sign. No, I suppose I'm just a troublemaker, a professional malcontent. I hate the system for lots of reasons— some of them big, a lot of them probably petty. No profit in citing chapter and verse. If I weren't with the Children, I would be throwing bombs with someone else. This seems a somewhat cleaner cause, that's all. You know, you are probably saner than I am, pantheism or not. I have worked in enough of those places like the one we just left that I picked up some of the jargon, some of the ideas, seen a lot of the cases. I sometimes think a lot of it applies to me." He laughed. "Then on even-numbered days," he went on, "I am sure it is the world that is mad and all that therapy would ever do is make me as batty as the rest of them."

I chuckled. We finished our cigarettes. I listened for sounds from outside the truck and tried to estimate where we might be. I heard nothing but the vehicle's own noises, though, and I had given up counting turns too long ago.

"We never figured out how they managed to locate you as fast as they did," Quick said. "Any ideas?"

"No."

"Well, this time we are being even more careful. If they do not catch up with us during the first hour or so we should be clear."

I thought back to that day, to the voice I thought I had heard. *Are you there now? Is it your will?* I wondered. But there was no answer.

After a time, we slowed and began to jounce about. I assumed we had left the road. We continued in this fashion for several minutes, then came to a halt.

I heard the cab door. A little later, the driver opened the rear of the truck. Looking out, I saw that we were on a dirt road, drawn up beside an arroyo.

I gestured with the pistol.

"All right, you two," I said. "Time to say goodbye."

The men got to their feet, moved back. I followed them and watched as they climbed down.

The older man looked back. For a moment, I thought he was going to say something, but he turned away and headed down the arroyo with the other.

The driver grinned after them.

"There go a couple scared hombres," he said.

"How much longer till we change over?"

He glanced at his watch.

"Five minutes," he said, and he closed the door.

I guess it was that. It seemed only about that long when we had drawn up again, gotten out and were climbing into a passenger vehicle drawn up at the side of the road. Quick and I got into the back. The truck's driver left his vehicle and climbed into the front with the new driver

We were back on the road in a matter of seconds, with nothing else in sight. It was open country all around us, and I was not certain exactly where we were, not that it mattered. We moved fast.

I was beginning to feel safe when we passed Cornudo Hills and took a turn to the northwest. I judged it had been about an hour since we had left the hospital. I felt some of the tension go out of me even as I wondered whether my absence had yet been noted. Even if it had, the trail was already beginning to cloud. More miles, more time . . .

Another half-hour and I was beginning to think we could make it. It was then that the driver spotted the police.

"Cops back of us," he announced. "They are not coming fast or blinking, though. Might just be a normal patrol."

"Might not, too," Quick said, leaning to the side and looking up. "Nothing in the sky, though," he added. "Of course, that doesn't prove anything, not when the terrain's this irregular. A flier could be circling anywhere, waiting for a car to call it in. If they are onto the break, cars will be alert all over the area and the fliers making regular passes."

"He's picked up a little speed," the driver said. "Gaining on us. Should I try to run for it?"

"No," I said. "That will draw attention. It may be nothing."

I rolled down the window.

"If they stop us and find that gun," Quick said, "they will take a closer look and they'll be bound to recognize you. So you might as well be ready to use it."

"I know," I said.

"Getting closer," the driver said.

"Any weapons in sight?" I asked.

"No. Not that that proves anything. There is a gun under my seat, too. Anybody want it?"

"Pass it here," Quick said. "Between the seats, not up where they can see it."

The driver leaned forward, straightened. Quick took the pistol from his hand.

"They are moving out to pass now. Maybe they will just go by."

Seconds later, I heard the siren.

I turned. They were right alongside us. Nothing to lose now. I fired twice at the right front tire and hit it.

"Go!" I shouted.

We did. There was gunfire behind us and the rear

window was broken, but Quick and I were already crouched. None of us was hurt.

When I looked back shortly thereafter, the patrol car was drawn up by the side of the road. A dip, a curve, and they were out of sight.

"They're on the radio by now," our former driver said.

"Sure," the present driver said. "It shouldn't be too long now and they'll be on us from the air. Any suggestions?"

"We don't know how far away the nearest flier is," Quick said. "It could be several minutes off."

"So? Catch us now or catch us in a couple minutes—what difference does it make?"

"So, we keep going. No sense trying to get out of sight if they know we're here. They would just block off the roads, bring in a lot of men and start beating the bushes. Keep going till we actually see a flier."

"By then it's too late."

"Maybe not. There are four of us in here. They can't tell who's who from the air. When we see the thing, you pull over. One of us gets out and takes off. The rest keep going. What'll they do?"

"I don't know. Chase the man and call for another flier maybe."

"Great. There can't be another one too close by. We gain a lot of distance. They close again, we drop another. That might be enough for you and Rod to make it. If not, you drop him and keep going. For all they know, he's driving. —Rod, it looks as if you might get that chance to live off the land pretty soon."

"Maybe so," I said.

"Who goes first?" the other driver asked.

"I don't care," Quick said. "Is there more ammo for this piece?"

"Yeah, almost a full box."

"Pass it back."

It came.

"Wait a minute," our previous driver said. "I'll go first. If you are figuring on shooting it out with them, I don't want to be second—armed or unarmed. I wouldn't have a chance. Drop me first and I'll give them a good run for it. Then if you get a turn at it, do whatever you want."

"Okay, fair enough."

"Those .38 longs?" I asked him.

"Yep."

"Then give me a dozen or so," I said.

"Check."

He pulled a handful and passed them over. I dropped them in my pocket.

Quick continued his survey of the sky.

"Nothing yet," he said. "Wonder how they found us so fast? Think they picked up those two dockhands? Or just luck?"

I shrugged.

"Doesn't much matter now," I said.

"No."

It was several miles—and again, I was almost beginning to believe we might make it—when Quick caught sight of the flier, topping a range of hills, dropping, coming in low.

"Okay, this is it," he said. "Pull over."

We did, and the other driver scrambled out.

"Luck," I said.

"Thanks."

He took off, sliding and running down the hillside off the road's shoulder.

"What was his name, anyway?" I asked as we moved forward again.

"Bob," Quick said. "That's all I know."

The pilot of the flier could not seem to make up his mind at first. He took the craft up higher and began circling. I suppose he could see Bob and us both at his new altitude.

"Keeping an eye on us while he calls for instructions," Quick said. "Bet they tell him to chase Bob."

"I don't suppose our next changeover is any too soon," I said.

"Sorry," said the driver. "I wish it were, too. Listen, they know where we are right now. If we stay on this drag, they'll box us in. What say I try a side road? I am not familiar with them around here, though. Are either of you?"

"No."

"No."

"What do you think?" he asked.

"Go ahead," I told him. "Pick a good one."

But there were no decent turnoffs for the next five or six miles. The flier, true to Quick's prediction, had finally dropped and vanished. I imagined that cars from Taos would be heading down the road toward us now.

"Better make it the first one that comes up," I said.

He nodded.

"I think I see it now."

He slowed as we approached it. It led down to the right. It was surfaced, but years overdue for maintenance.

It slowed us, but I heard myself sigh after the first mile or so. It did not peter out, did not worsen. There was no one in sight, anywhere.

The sun still had a long way to go. On foot, after dark, my chances might be better, I decided.

"I don't suppose there's a canteen of water aboard?" I asked.

The driver chuckled.

"Afraid not," he said. "I wasn't figuring on anything but taxi service."

"Next time you'll know better," I said. "Pull over by those trees up ahead and drop me off."

"Okay."

"That is not the plan," Quick said.

"No, but it's a better one," I said. "If I can stay out of sight till after dark I can do a lot of hiking before morning."

We reached the trees, came to a halt.

"See you around," I said.

I got out and headed away. The driver called something after me. It sounded like "Good luck."

It was minutes later and some distance from there that I heard the flier. I was under the trees, on the ground, motionless, in a moment. I did not even look up. I just waited for it to pass.

71

But it did not.

The sounds of its engines reached a maximum and held there. Finally, I looked up. It was circling.

Damn! Why? It had not been in sight when I had gotten out. It should be looking for the car. Unless ... I spat out some dust. Unless they had a personnel detector of some sort—infrared, a heat spotter—and were scanning the area, had picked up my outline.

Yes, that had to be it. The flier was beginning to descend.

The thing was dropping toward a clearing several hundred meters off to my right. As soon as it had dropped below treetop level, I was on my feet and heading off into the trees in the opposite direction. It was not a large stand of wood, but when I emerged I saw where another began across a rock-strewn slope of Russian thistle and chamisa, about a quarter-mile away. I began running toward it. I grew short of breath sooner than I had thought I might. Despite daily calisthenics, my months of confinement had softened me.

I forced myself, breathing heavily, and did not look back. Before I reached the trees, I heard a voice on a bullhorn: "Halt! This is the police!"

I kept running.

"You are covered! We will shoot! Halt!"

The first one would be a warning shot, I figured, and the next would not be all that accurate. I was dizzy and my thighs were beginning to hurt, but I was not about to halt.

I heard the first shot.

"That was a warning! Halt!"

There followed several more and I heard them ricocheting nearby. I was not going to make it to the trees, I realized. I felt on the verge of passing out. There were some rocks ahead, though. . . .

More gunfire . . .

I dove for the rocks, collapsed behind them, lay there panting.

I expected another challenge, but none came. The gunfire rattled on, but none of it seemed to be coming anywhere near me. I peered around the side of the rock.

There were four police, three of them in prone firing positions shooting back into the trees I had departed, the fourth sprawled on his back, his limbs positioned unnaturally.

I panted until my head cleared, studying the situation before me. Shortly, I realized that their fire was being returned. Who . . . ?

Of course. It was Quick. It had to be. He had waited till I was out of sight and followed me, the stupid ass. Now he was trying to delay them, in order to buy me time. Only he was likely to get himself killed with such damnfoolery. My escape was not worth his life. I would as soon go back and do some time as see him get shot over it. I would still be alive. I would get out one day. . . .

It seemed from the fire pattern that he was moving around in the wood. As I watched, trying to figure where he was, another of the figures before me jerked and lay still.

Two remaining . . . They would never take him back alive after this. The fight would go on to a finish, and it could only end one way. Pretty soon now, too. He could not have much more ammo.

I found the pistol in my hand. Neither of them was looking my way. They must have assumed that I had kept going when the diversion began. I got to my feet. Crouched, I began jogging toward them, ready to throw myself flat the moment one turned. I kept telling myself it was not that bad a risk. There were more rocks up near where they lay. If I could make it that far we would have them in a crossfire and it would not take that long to finish things.

As I neared, the firing from the trees ceased. Quick had seen me, did not want to risk catching me with a stray shot. All right. I had covered half the distance back. . . .

I suppose that at first the police thought they had hit him. The thought even crossed my mind. Still, the coincidence of my approach made my first guess seem

73

more likely. They did not move. They retained their positions and held their fire, perhaps also expecting a ruse to get them to expose themselves. I kept running. I was almost within range.

It was this silence, I suppose, that undid me. The man on my right must have caught some sound of my approach. He turned his head, looked back.

Automatically, I dove forward, fixed both elbows, propped my right hand with my left and began firing.

He had turned by then and swung his rifle about. If I did not nail him quickly . . .

On my third shot he slumped, getting off one round, wildly, into the air.

Then I felt a searing pain in my chest and I slumped forward, triggering one unaimed shot in the direction of the second man just before my head hit the ground and I tasted blood and dirt.

Then there was more gunfire. It had a distant sound to it. Everything seemed distant. I struggled to raise my head, propped it on a tower of fists. As through a shrinking tunnel, I saw that a man had emerged from the trees, shooting. It was Quick. The final officer, who had risen to one knee, had swiveled from my direction to that of the wood and was returning the fire. Even as I watched, he toppled and Quick kept coming.

I slumped again, blackness beating about my head. Was it for this? The extra few months I had gained— what end had they served? I could as soon have bought it that morning in Santa Fe. . . . But the trial, the publicity— Yes. That voice I once had heard . . . half-drunk, so late. . . . Real? No difference, I suppose, old Mother. . . . Unto thee . . . Sorry about that last cigarette. I— Are you there? Is it truly . . . ?"

I have never left you.

It is well. . . .

Come to me.

I—

Dennis Guise was catatonic once again. He lay on his bed staring at nothing. He soiled himself and had to be changed like a baby. When Lydia placed food in his

74

mouth, he chewed and swallowed mechanically, giving no indication that he was aware of the process. He no longer spoke, beyond an occasional muttering late at night as he slept. He did not walk about.

Yet Lydia claimed there had been progress, that he had benefited from his association with the slain assassin Roderick Leishman, that locked now within his subconscious were the necessary ingredients for the personality he would one day develop, driven deep by the trauma of the death he had witnessed.

A month passed. And a week.

One cool Tuesday morning when Vicki rose and went to the kitchen, she found the coffee already made. A cup of it steamed on the breakfast bar at the left hand of her son, who, fully dressed, sat smoking and reading the paper.

". . . Goddamn pollutocrats," he muttered, "at it again!"

He glanced up at her. He slapped the paper against the counter, raised it and waved it at her.

"Look what that damn crowd down south is up to," he said. "Fouling the ocean! You'd think they'd want their own fishing industry to—"

Vicki uttered a short shriek, turned and fled.

Shortly thereafter, Lydia, in a green and orange flower-print robe, came to the kitchen and took coffee with him. That evening, having directed soothing impulses through his sleep centers, she left him snoring in his room and went and looked at the stars for a time.

Vicki felt after her mind, but there was nothing there for several minutes. Finally, Lydia came into the house, darkness beneath her eyes.

"I was just going to have a drink," Vicki said. "Would you care for one?"

"Please. Some of your husband's scotch, over ice."

Lydia drank slowly, her eyes on nothing in the room.

"He has, obviously, done it again," she began. "He has located a new personality and occupied it completely. This time it is a man known as Smith,

Quick Smith, an associate of Leishman's who was apparently with him fairly near the end—"

"Should we notify the authorities again?"

"No. It would serve no useful purpose. The case is closed. Leishman and four police found dead in a field, the result of a gun battle. It is over now. True, this man knew him. What of it? That is no crime. Let it go at that. Besides, I have no real idea where he is anyhow. His mind is much harder to get into via this route than Leishman's ever was. A touch of the psychotic there, but that is all right. He is far from here, that much I know, and not up to any harm. Dennis must have picked him up through their association, near to the end, and only recently recovered sufficiently to pursue the connection."

"What will this one lead to?"

"A dead end, I fear. I believe there is already sufficient material stored within him for me to continue the structuring we spoke of. But this blocks it. So long as there is a fresh personality intervening I cannot get at it. Nor do I wish to try it with this new personality, so long as the rapport exists."

"What then are we to do?"

Lydia raised her glass, took a drink, lowered it.

"I spent the entire day seeking the key to this thing," she said, "and when I finally located it, I was too tired to turn it. I believe that I can break this new connection."

"How?"

"Mainly by blocking him for a while. I believe that if I frustrate him here, he will withdraw again."

"Mightn't that hurt him?"

"No. It will just put him back where he was, so that I can continue working with him. The only reason I did not do it today is that it will call for more stamina than I could muster by the time I figured how to go about it. He is extremely strong. I have never encountered a telepath with that kind of power before."

"But might he not just reach out and reestablish the connection after you take the pressure off?"

"I do not think so. Not right away, anyhow. Look

how long he remained withdrawn after Leishman's death."

"True. When are you going to try?"

"Tomorrow, if I am up to it. I feel that I will be."

"Do you want to talk with Dr. Winchell first?"

"Not really. This is my area of specialization, not his. He would leave the decision to me, and since I have already made it a consultation would be redundant."

"All right. Shall we tell Dick?"

"Not yet. This is not really so crucial a point as it may seem. It is just a repetition of the earlier business. Why disturb him when we have nothing significant to report? Wait until there is some real progress."

Vicki nodded. They finished their drinks and talked of other things.

The following day, with some difficulty, Lydia succeeded in breaking Dennis' contact with the man called Smith. As she had anticipated, he returned once more to his catatonic state. But now, his tendency to mutter in his sleep was greater, and he began having occasional spells of somnambulism. Vicki once saw him move past her door and followed, to find him seated in the courtyard staring at the moon. When she led him back to his bed he did not awaken, though she thought he whispered "Mother" as they went.

After two weeks, he was a truck driver named Ingalls, on the road, heading toward El Paso. Lydia broke the contact immediately and continued therapy. He now occasionally muttered unconnected phrases while in a waking state. His sleepwalking became an almost nightly affair, though he never went beyond the courtyard.

A week later, he was a pilot en route to Los Angeles. Lydia broke the contact and attempted to direct his attention to things about him.

Four days later, he was a mining engineer in Montana. Lydia broke the contact and began taking him on walks, as she could now stimulate motor areas of his brain which had apparently undergone some development in the course of his various contacts. Still, it seemed close to his somnambulism, as his mind remained vague throughout the course of the strolling.

Three days later, he was a crewman aboard a cargo vessel somewhere south of Hawaii. Lydia broke the contact and began playing music in his presence.

Two days after that, he was a freshman listening to a guest speaker at a large Eastern university. Lydia broke the contact and put him to sleep.

The following day, he was an Austrian mountain climber somewhere in the Alps. Lydia broke the contact and took him for a walk. As they walked along a ridge to the east, he began speaking to her in Russian. She answered him in that language, then broke the contact and took him home.

Later that evening, he was the son of a farmer in northern India, and he went to the kitchen and began to eat. Lydia spoke with him softly for a time, in a speech full of labial consonants, and then gently broke the contact. She took him to his room then and caused him to sleep.

Lydia accepted more of Dick's scotch and went to sit on the floor before the corner fireplace, shoes off, hair loose, eyes turning liquid in the flamelight.

"What is happening?" Vicki said, coming up behind her, touching her.

"He is just beginning to feel what he can do," Lydia said, "such as reach anywhere in the world, regard anyone's thoughts with total absorption—a vicarious pleasure, and easier than developing his own personality. So long as he is about this, this—vampirism—therapy remains at a standstill."

"What are you going to do?"

"Keep blocking him. Try to implant a suggestion against this sort of behavior. Keep directing his attention to local stimuli."

"Will that be sufficient?"

Lydia sipped her drink, turned and stared into the flames. At length, she spoke, "I do not know. You see, it gets more difficult each time, now that he is growing aware of his power. I have succeeded in blocking him each time by means of technique, not strength. Just today, for the first time, he resisted me slightly. I do not know how much longer it will be before this becomes an active thing. If it should, I will not be able to block him."

"What then?"

"It may not come to that. The suggestion may work. If it does not . . . Then I suppose I would have to try another technique. Say, render him unconscious and apply the block immediately as he begins to come out of it. That may work. . . ."

"And if it does not . . . ?"

"We should know fairly soon," Lydia said.

That night, Dennis made his way to the courtyard and began singing in Italian. Lydia spoke to him in Italian, led him back to his room, returned him to sleep and reinforced the suggestion she had implanted earlier. In the morning, she took him for a walk while the chill still lay on the land. She showed him the sunrise and spoke with him at length. He mumbled inappropriate responses. They returned to the house, where she fed him and played more music.

That afternoon, Dennis assumed the personality of a Japanese policeman. She chatted with him in a singsong fashion for some twenty minutes before gently applying the block that was to break the contact. This time, Dennis resisted more actively. She succeeded in breaking the contact, attempted another reinforcement of the suggestion, went and called Vicki to join her for tea.

"It is not working," she said, "and his resistance to the blocking has increased. It will not be too long before I am unable to contain him. He does not seem to be accepting the suggestions. I will try the sleep approach next time. I feel, though, that he will learn to resist it also."

"Would it help to have Dr. Winchell prescribe some drug? A tranquilizer, perhaps? Something to slow him down, make him easier to control?"

Lydia shook her head.

"It would interfere with the therapy to have him doped up."

"But what else is there to do?"

"I do not know. I had not anticipated this development."

"If we were to move again, someplace out of range . . . ?"

"He is able to reach all around the world now. There is no escape that way."

"I had better see if I can reach Dick—and then Dr. Winchell."

Lydia nodded.

"Go ahead."

Now it happened that Dick's current mistress was a public information officer for Moonbase II. That evening, as Dick sat drinking in her apartment overlooking the Potomac, he told her of the latest report on his son's condition.

"Is there a pattern?" she asked him. "Some common trait shared by all the minds he has occupied?"

"Yes," he said. "I thought to ask Lydia about that, and she told me that all of them were, in some way, eco nuts. Not necessarily COE, but environmentalists and reformers, active or passive."

"Interesting," she said. "If there were none of them available, I wonder what he would do?"

Dick shrugged.

"Who can say, Sue? Withdraw completely, once more? Or find someone else to focus on? No way of telling."

She came over and rubbed his shoulders.

"Then you've got to get him out of range," she said, "to someplace where there are very few people, and where those there are have little time to think of these problems with the same immediacy of concern."

Dick chuckled.

"You do not understand," he said. "He can reach anywhere in the world. Here he is, the greatest telepath alive, and it is his ability that is screwing him. Here I am, the father of the greatest telepath alive, and I can get him anything—anything except the switch that will

80

turn him off long enough for them to straighten him out."

"The moon," she said, "is around a quarter of a million miles away."

He turned and looked into her eyes. He began to smile, then he shook his head.

"It wouldn't work," he said. "There is no way. . . ."

"There are two hospitals there," she said. "I know all the people involved. You carry a lot of weight. I could tell you which strings to pull."

"How do we know it will do any good?"

"What is the alternative? Your therapist admits that she cannot control him any longer. Send him to the moon where there is very little interference. Let their psych teams have a try."

Dick took a large swallow and closed his eyes.

"I'm thinking," he said.

She moved around, seated herself in the chair across from him. He reached out and took her hand.

"Are you reading my mind?" she finally said.

"No. Should I?"

"I don't think you have to."

He smiled and stood. She rose to meet him.

"You're full of good ideas," he said. "I think I'll try both of them."

Part III

The facility lay within a small crater in the southern lunar hemisphere. Cleaned-out, built-up, domed-over, air-conditioned, nuclear-powered, fountained, ponded, treed, painted, furnished and filled with the small noises of life, it was home to a great number of wealthy geriatric patients whose conditions precluded their ever returning to the bluegreen ball in the dark sky, save to dwell within it. It was not noted as a psychiatric facility save in the areas of senile dementia and arteriosclerotic brain disease.

The new patient, a teenage boy, sat on a bench near a fountain, as he did every day at the same time. A therapist, Alec Stern, sat beside him reading a book, as he did every day at the same time. If Alec were to reach out and move the boy's arm into a new position, it would remain there. If he were to ask him a question, more often than not it would be met with silence. Occasionally, though, it would be answered with an inappropriate muttering. As today:

"Pretty, isn't it—the way the colors dance on the water?" Alec asked, lowering his book for a moment.

The boy, whose head was turned in that direction, said, "Flowers . . ."

"It reminds you of the colors of flowers? Yes, that is true. Any special kind?"

Silence.

Alec withdrew a notebook from his pocket and scribbled in it.

"Would you like to walk with me and look at some flowers?"

Silence.

"Come on, then."

He placed the book on the bench and took the boy's arm. There was no resistance as he drew him to his feet. Once he started him moving he kept walking, mechanically. He steered him around the fountain and up a walkway, coming quickly to the area of controlled lighting where the flowerbeds lay.

"See. Tulips," he said, "and daffodils. Reds, yellows, oranges. You like them?"

Nothing.

"You want to touch one?"

He took the boy's hand, pushed him forward, brushed his fingertips against the red petals of a huge tulip.

"Soft," he said, "isn't it? Do you like it?"

The boy remained bent forward. He helped him to straighten.

"Come on. Let's go back."

He took hold of his arm once again and led him down the walkway.

Later, after the boy had been fed and put to rest in his room, Alec spoke with Dr. Chalmers.

"The boy," Dr. Chalmers said, "Dennis?"

"No change. Moves only with assistance. An occasional word."

"But inside? What is his mind doing? What are his reactions to the new environment?"

"Nothing special. He is barely aware of the change. He is a collection of pieces, most of them submerged, surfacing in a random fashion, sinking again—flashes here and there, occasional interactions. Most of them a matter of personal preoccupation."

"Do you feel we ought to shift to brain stimulation?"

Alec shook his head.

"No. I would like to continue along the lines suggested by his former therapist. She was getting results near the end. Things just developed too suddenly for her to keep control in the saturation environment down there." He gestured vaguely overhead. "She foresaw a dormant period such as this following his transfer. But she also felt that the experiences he has undergone would then cause him to come out of it and seek new stimulation after a time."

"Well, it has been almost a month."

"Her guess was a month to six weeks."

"And you buy that?"

"She was good. I can see the results of her work whenever I am with him. I do not understand everything that she did. But there is some sort of effect, almost a kind of cyclical sequencing in the recurrence of imprinted personality aspects. I think we are safest in sticking with her program for now. I still do not know as much about the boy as she did. Too bad she could not have stayed on."

"Something about a divorce and her not wanting to take sides. She was in favor of the boy's transfer up here, though."

"Yeah, a certain amount of it is in Dennis' mind. Very low-key, though. And I've always been an admirer of his old man, so I am prejudiced. Whatever, it is not really material to Dennis' problem."

"I have to send Mr. Guise a report this week. I wish you would stop around the office after lunch and give me a hand with it. He wants one every month."

"Okay. By next time, we may have something more positive to say."

It was almost two weeks later that Alec went to fetch him in the morning and found Dennis crouched on the floor, tracing geometric designs with a forefinger moistened with saliva. Dennis did not seem aware of Alec's entry into the cell, so Alec stood by the door, watching. After a time, he extended his awareness, slowly, carefully. But he was unable to get beyond the most intense concentration he had ever encountered, a concentration focused entirely on the properties of triangles.

For the better part of an hour he stood there, fascinated by the action, the concentration, hoping to be noticed. Finally, he moved forward.

When he stood behind him, he reached out and touched Dennis' shoulder.

The boy turned suddenly and looked up at him. It

was the first time he had seen those eyes focus, the first time he had witnessed anything resembling intelligence in the way that they moved, in the expression which accompanied their regard.

Then Dennis screamed—a sentence or two. And then he collapsed, falling forward across his moist diagrams.

Alec raised him in his arms and carried him to the bed. He deposited him upon it and checked his heartbeat, his pulse. Both were rapid. He drew up the chair and seated himself at the bedside.

As he waited for Dennis to regain consciousness, the sounds of that scream still echoed within his awareness. He had shouted in a foreign language—he was sure of that. The sounds were too regular, too organized, to be random gibberish. Alec had not recognized the tongue, but he was certain it was a bona fide patterned utterance. Everything else about the boy's attitude—his actions, his concentration, his expression—had been informed with too much purposefulness for the picture to fall apart when it came to the vocalization. When Dennis awakened, it should not be too difficult to determine what lunar mind he had invaded. . . .

But it was a long while before Dennis awakened, and when he did his eyes regarded nothing in particular and his mind was almost as it had been the day before. Only the faintest hint of some recent contact remained, a tone, a touch of mood, indefinable, which had not been present previously. Nothing more, nothing of sufficient substantiality to permit an identification.

Alec led him out, for a walk about the compound, attempting to apply neural emphasis to various sensory effects, with the usual results. He finally led him back to the bench by the fountain. It was there that he decided to attempt an exercise based on the recent phenomenon he had witnessed.

Opening his notebook to a blank page, he sketched a triangle, a circle, a square. Then he thrust the notebook before Dennis and held it there.

After a time, Dennis lowered his head. His eyes focused, moved. He reached out and took the notebook in his hands. He moved it to his lap and bent above it. He traced the figures' outlines with his forefinger.

"What are they?" Alex said. "Can you tell me what they are?"

Dennis' lips moved. He whispered, "Circle, square, triangle . . ."

"Excellent! Here." Alec thrust his pencil into his hand. "Can you draw more?"

Dennis stared at the pencil, then handed it back. He shook his head. He leaned forward again, outlined the figures once more with his finger, then looked away. The notebook slid from his lap and fell to the ground. He did not seem to notice.

"What are they?" Alec said. "Can you tell me again?"

Dennis did not reply. His thoughts were shifting in random patterns once more.

Alec retrieved the notebook and began writing.

Dennis' condition remained unchanged for most of a week following this. Attempts were made to interest him in various of the recreative and rehabilitative classes available, and though he began paying attention to music he had no apparent desire to learn to play an instrument. Entered in an art class, he confined himself to the drawing of circles, triangles and squares. His skill in reproducing these figures freehanded soon reached a state of near-mechanical perfection. His conversational abilities were restricted to a word or two—three at most—in response to numerous and simply phrased repetitions of simple questions. He never initiated a conversation.

All of this, however, could be taken as considerable improvement, and was. The next report sent to his parents indicated progress in manual, verbal and ideational skills. What it did not include was the French episode and its aftermath.

When Alec went to fetch him one morning, he found Dennis pacing back and forth in his room, muttering in French. On attempting to speak with him, he received replies only in French. Probing telepathically, he discovered a new identity pattern. He left Dennis pacing and went in search of a young French physician recently assigned to the facility.

Marcel spent the entire afternoon with Dennis and came away with a sheaf of notes.

"He believes he is the Marquis de Condorcet," he announced later that evening, arranging the notes on his desk and looking up at Alec. "In fact, he almost convinced me of it."

"What do you mean?" Alec said.

"He possesses incredible amounts of information about the Marquis' life—and the times."

"It could be something like an idiot savant function," Alec offered. "Something he heard, something he absorbed long ago from some mind he touched, just now surfacing."

"But it is fully consistent, Alec, and he did more than repeat facts. He engaged in intelligent—extremely intelligent—conversation. He was talking about his— rather, the Marquis'—*Sketch for a Historical Picture of the Progress of the Human Mind*. He did not just recite the points. He answered questions and he expanded on the thoughts which exist in the essay itself. It is more than fanciful utopianism, you know. He went on about the perfection of man as a consequence of the diffusion of knowledge, about science as a way of mind which would raise the material level of mankind as well as enhance the intellect of the individual, about—"

"A moment," Alec said, raising his hand. "We have already established that he is not oriented with respect to person and time. What about place, though? How did he justify being on the moon and in late-eighteenth-century France simultaneously?"

Marcel smiled.

"A cell is a cell," he said. "The Marquis spent his last days in prison. That is where he thought he was."

"Victim of the Revolution, wasn't he?"

"Yes. Though it is still a debatable point whether he was executed or took his own life rather than—"

Alec stiffened.

"What—?" Marcel began.

"I don't know. But that bothers me. Whatever the source of his information, that might be there."

"Surely you do not think . . . ?"

Alec stood.

"I am going to check on him. It troubles me."

"I'll come with you."

They strode across the compound.

"He has never exhibited any—tendencies—in that direction, has he?"

"Not since he has been here," Alec said, "and there is nothing in the record to that effect. But the way his personality reshuffles itself, it is difficult to guess what he might be like at any given time. My God!"

"What?"

"I'm reading him!"

Alec broke into a run.

They reached Dennis' room to find him on the floor. Using his belt, he had attempted to hang himself from a light fixture. The fixture, however, had given way. Unconscious, he lay beside the chair on which he had stood to make the arrangements.

Marcel checked him quickly.

"His neck does not seem broken," he said, "but I want X-rays. Go get something to transport him. I will stay here."

"Right."

A thorough examination showed that Dennis had sustained no major injuries. It did not show why he had entered a coma, in which he remained for over two days. During this time, he remained in the clinic being fed from a dripping bottle, monitored by observers human and mechanical.

When on the third day he awakened, Dennis clutched at his side and moaned. A nurse appeared, observed his distress and sent for a doctor. A gross examination showed nothing amiss, and more elaborate test were undertaken. While their results were being considered, Marcel and Alec arrived at the bedside and determined that Dennis was no longer the Marquis de Condorcet. A telepathic examination revealed that he believed himself lying in a meadow near a rocky outcrop, bleeding from a wound inflicted by the horn of a fabulous beast from the sea. He also felt that his former therapist Lydia Dimanche was with him and frequently addressed the attending nurse by her name.

"All the tests are negative," said an older doctor who had come into the room during the TP scan.

"It is another of his—delusions," Alec said. "There are instructions in his file for breaking something like this. I think it would help if he had a sedative."

"I don't know," the older doctor said. "He has been out for quite some time. He is weak. . . . What about a simple relaxant?"

"All right. Let's try that."

The doctor sent for the necessary drug, administered an injection. The nurse held Dennis' hand. After a few minutes, a certain tension seemed to go out of him. His moans grew weaker, ceased. Alec moved then, carefully, firmly, to break a hypothetical connection. The mind he regarded suddenly swam, then drifted. Dennis closed his eyes and his breathing grew regular. The doctor moved to take his pulse.

"A normal sleep, I'd say," he announced half a minute later. "You found a way to separate him from the anxiety source?"

"I guess that is as good a way to put it as any. Yes. Unless he comes up with something new awfully fast he should be his old self when he awakens—if he sticks to what seems the pattern he has been following."

"Then the best thing we can do is let him sleep right now—and keep the monitors on." He regarded the flashboard. "His functions are well above the previous coma level."

Alec nodded.

"It seems best. Have them call me right away, though, if there are any changes in his condition."

"Of course," the doctor said.

They went away and left him sleeping.

On awakening, Dennis seemed returned to his more innocuous, earlier self. He walked with Alec about the facility, regarding with slightly enhanced attention those objects presented to him. He considered the flowers in the gardens and the stars beyond the dome, the Earth far away. His communicative abilities grew slowly during the weeks that followed, though he still did not initiate conversations, did not ask questions.

Dennis returned to his art class. He continued to draw geometric figures, but now he began embellishing them, and surrounding them with curlicues and elaborate filigree work. The hard, decisive lines he had originally drawn were softened in the basic figures and more of an element of freehand became apparent in the elaborations.

Alec then decided it was time to ask him, "What is your name?"

Dennis did not answer him, but continued staring at the atmosphere regulation plant across the way from where they were seated.

Alec rested his hand on his shoulder.

"Your name?" he repeated softly. "Would you tell me your name?"

"Name—" Dennis whispered. "Name—"

"*Your* name. What is it?"

Dennis' eyes narrowed, his brows lowered, tightened. He began to breathe rapidly.

Alec squeezed his shoulder.

"It is all right. It is all right," he said. "I will just tell you. Your name is Dennis. Dennis Guise."

The signs of tension vanished. Dennis sighed.

"Can you say it? Can you say Dennis Guise?"

"Dennis," Dennis said. "Dennis Guise."

"Good! Very good," Alec told him. "If you can remember that you will be doing well."

They walked on.

About fifteen minutes later, Alec asked him, "Now, what is your name?"

Dennis' face took on a look of anguish. Again, his breathing increased.

"We talked about it just a little while ago," Alec said. "Try to remember."

Dennis began to cry.

"It is all right," Alec said, taking his arm. "It is Dennis Guise. Dennis Guise. That is all."

Dennis gasped, sighed. He said nothing.

The next day he did not recall it, and Alec abandoned the problem of identity establishment for the time being. Dennis showed no ill effects from the small trauma.

Several days passed, and then the instructor of the art class noticed a totally incongruous sketch on Dennis' pad. His pencil was moving to the completion of an amazing caricature of one of the other students.

"That is extremely good," she remarked. "I was not aware that you did faces."

Dennis glanced up at her and smiled. It was the first time she had ever seen him smile.

"When did you begin using your left hand?"

He performed a palms-up gesture with both hands and shrugged.

Later, the instructor showed some of the new drawings to Alec.

Alec whistled.

"Was there anything leading up to this sort of work?" he asked.

"No. It happened quite suddenly, along with his switching hands."

"He's a southpaw now?"

"Yes. I thought you would be interested in that—as an indication of some neurological development, perhaps—a possible shifting of control from one brain hemisphere to the other—"

"Yes, thanks," he said. "I'll have Jefferson, over in neuropsych, check him over again. Were there any behavioral shifts accompanying this?"

She nodded.

"But it is hard to put a finger on it," she said. "It is just that he seems more—more animated—now, and there is an alert look, something about the way he moves his eyes, that was not there before."

"I had better go see him right now," Alec said. "Thanks again."

He made his way to Dennis' quarters, knocked and reached to open the door.

"Yes?" said a voice from within.

"It's me—Alec," he said. "May I come in?"

"Come in," said the voice, without inflection.

Dennis was seated by the window, sketchpad open on his lap. He looked up and smiled as Alec entered.

Alec approached, glanced down at the pad. It was filled with sketches of nearby buildings.

"Very good," he said. "I am glad to see that you are moving on to other subject matter."

Dennis smiled again.

"You seem to be in good spirits today. I am glad about that, too. Any special reason?"

Dennis shrugged.

"Say," Alec said, almost casually. "I didn't mean to trouble you the other day with that business about your name."

"No—trouble," Dennis said.

"*Do* you recall it, though?"

"Say—it—again."

"Dennis. Dennis Guise."

"Yes. Dennis Guise. Yes."

"Care for a little exercise?"

"Exer—cise?"

"Would you like to go for your walk now?"

"Oh. Yes. Yes. A walk. Exercise . . ."

Dennis closed the pad. He rose and crossed the room. He opened the door, held it for Alec.

Alec led him along their usual route toward the fountain.

"Anything special you would like to talk about?" he asked.

"Yes," Dennis immediately replied. "Talk about talk."

"I—I don't quite understand."

"Talk—ing. Parts."

"Words?"

"Yes. Words."

"Oh. You want to review your vocabulary. All right. Sure."

Alec began naming everything they passed. Suppressing excitement, he reviewed the parts of the body, pronouns, basic verbs. Dennis' speech blossomed as they strolled.

Later, standing beside the fountain, Dennis asked, "How does it work, the fountain?"

"Oh, just a simple pump," Alex said.

"What sort of pump? I would like to see it."

"I am not certain exactly what kind of pump it is. I can speak with someone in maintenance later and probably get you a look at it. Maybe tomorrow."

"All right. Sure. Alec?"

"What?"

"I— Where are we?"

"This is the Luna Medical Facility II."

"Luna!"

"Yes, the moon. You are only just beginning to realize . . . ?"

Dennis had sagged back against the side of the fountain. Suddenly, he looked up.

"No overhead views from this section," Alec said. "If you would like, I can take you to an observation deck."

Dennis nodded vigorously.

"Please."

Alec took his arm.

"I guess that it would come as a shock—if you had not realized it, had not thought about it, all along. I should apologize. I am taking too many things for granted, because of the way you suddenly began communicating since you—since you . . ."

". . . became less mad?" Dennis finished, recovering his composure and smiling.

"No, no. That is the wrong word. Listen, do you have any understanding, of what has been happening to you, of what things have been like for you until today?"

Dennis shook his head.

"Not really," he said. "I wish that I did."

Alec tried a quick mental probe, but as on two earlier occasions during their walk that day, he could not get beyond the surface thoughts, forcused as they were on present circumstances with such force of concentration as to preclude access to anything beyond them.

"I see no reason not to tell you something about it," Alec said. "You have been ill much of your life with a condition brought on by your telepathic faculty. You were exposed to adult thoughts too soon—from birth—and they interfered with your own thinking, until now. Bringing you to the moon got you away from much of the interference. This has finally allowed you to achieve some stability, to sort things out, to begin to think for yourself, to become aware of who you are. Do you understand? You are just now beginning to come into your own as a rational being."

"I—think I see. The past is so cloudy . . ."

"Of course. The elevator is this way."

"What is a telepathic faculty?"

"Well . . . An ability to tell directly what other people are thinking."

"Oh."

"It was too much for a child to cope with."

"Yes."

"Do you have any idea what brought you out of it? Do you recall when your thoughts first came to include a measure of self-awareness?"

Dennis grinned.

"No. It is sort of like waking up," he said. "You are never certain when it begins, but there comes a time when it has occurred. I think it is still going on."

"Good."

Alec thumbed open a door, led Dennis within, pressed a button on the wall.

"I am—quite—ignorant," Dennis said. "Do not take it as a—relapse—if I ask about the obvious—or lack certain words."

"Lord, no! You are making progress right before my eyes. In fact, I find it difficult to believe this is really happening."

The elevator hummed about them. Dennis touched the wall and chuckled.

"So do I, so do I. Tell me, do you possess this—telepathic faculty—yourself?"

97

"Yes."

"Do many people?"

"No, we are a distinct minority."

"I see. Are you using yours on me?"

"No. I feel we are better off talking this way. The practice is good for you. Do you want to try the other?"

"Not just now. No."

"Good. I was coming to that. It may be better if you do not attempt it for a time. No sense running the risk of reopening old channels of vulnerability until you have toughened your psyche a bit more."

"That sounds reasonable."

The door opened. Alec led him out into the observation lounge—a long, curved room, chairs and benches spotted about it, lit only by the stars and the great globe of the Earth beyond the transparent bubble that roofed it.

Dennis gasped and flattened himself against the wall.

"It's all right," Alec said. "Safe. There is nothing to fear."

"Give me a chance," Dennis said. "Wait and let me look. Do not talk. God! It is lovely! Up there. The world . . . I have to paint it. How will I get the colors . . . here?"

"Ms. Brant will give you paints," Alec said.

"But the light . . ."

"There are alcoves farther along which can be illuminated—" He gestured. "You never realized . . . that all this was here? That this was where you were—the moon?"

"No. I—I want to sit in one of the chairs."

"Of course. Come on."

Alec led him to a pair of chairs, reclined them, saw Dennis into one, took the other himself. For perhaps an hour they regarded the sky. Alec tried probing Dennis twice during that time, but on both occasions was met with that fierce concentration which blocked further reading.

Finally, Dennis rose.

"It is almost too much," he said. "Let us go back now."

Alec nodded.

"Want to try eating in the cafeteria? Or would that be too much excitement for one day?"

"Let us try it and find out."

As they rode the elevator down, Alec remarked, "We will probably never know what specific thing it was that set off this improvement of yours."

"Probably not."

". . . And there are many things about it which I do not understand."

Dennis smiled.

". . . But the one that puzzles me the most is where you could have picked up an Italian accent."

"If you ever find out, tell me," Dennis said.

Dr. Timura could detect no signs of neurological dysfunction. His main remarks centered about Dennis' interest in the testing equipment and his questions concerning localizations of function within the brain. He spent half an hour more than he had intended with Dennis, going over neural anatomy charts.

"Whatever did it," he told Alec later, "it was something functional—and you are asking the wrong man when it comes to that. It is more your area than mine."

"I had figured it was," Alec said. "We actually know so little about telepaths. . . ."

"For whatever it is worth, it looks as if the idea behind his being sent here in the first place has proved valid. It got him away from the adverse stimuli, gave him a breather, he took advantage of it and now he is pulling himself together. It just took a while to have its effect."

"Yes, there is that. But to come this far from borderline sentience in one day is—remarkable. He's got paint and canvas and a box of tapes now. He is asking questions about everything—"

"Long-suppressed curiosity coming to the fore? For that matter, there is no way of knowing what his intelligence level really was. Quite high, I'd guess."

"Granted, granted. But what about the time he thought he was Condorcet?"

"He had to have picked that up through some use of his telepathic faculty. You will probably never know exactly where."

"I suppose you are right, but there is something peculiar about his present state of consciousness, also."

"What is that?"

"I can't read him. I am a pretty good telepath myself, or I would not have gone into TP therapy work. But every time I try a scan, I never get a millimeter beyond his immediate object of concern. He possesses the concentration of a tournament chess player—at all times. *That* is not normal."

"There *are* other people like that. Artists, for example, when they are wrapped up in a piece of work. And he *is* interested in art."

"True. For that matter, he is an extremely powerful telepath, and it may be some sort of unconscious block he has set up. Do you think he might be moving too fast now, heading for some sort of reaction?"

Dr. Timura shrugged.

"There will probably be a reaction of some sort. Depression . . . Fatigue certainly, if he keeps going the way that he is. On the other hand, it might be worse to try to head it off at this point, while he is trying to learn everything he can. When he gets his belly full he will quit and digest his gains. It will be after that that your real work will begin. That's just my opinion, of course."

"Thanks. I'm grateful for any advice on this case."

"You have monitors in his room, don't you?"

"Of course, ever since he came here—and a few extras since the incident when he was Condorcet."

"Good, good. Why don't you give him some more time to himself now—since he is covered on that front—and see what he makes of it?"

"You mean stop therapy and give him his head?"

"Nothing quite that radical. But you are going to want to observe him a while before you decide what course of therapy is now in order. You do not want to keep things as highly structured as when he was barely able to get around on his own, do you?"

"No. That is true. I guess I will lie low a bit and let the machines do the watching. I will just drop in on him later to see how the painting is going—and observe. I will see you."

"Take care."

Alec knocked on the door, waited.

"Yes?"

"It's me—Alec."

"Come on in."

He entered, to find Dennis seated on the bed, a portable viewer set up at his side. Across the room stood an easel bearing a completed canvas. It was the skyscape as seen from the deck, the Earth prominent within it. Alec moved to stand before it.

"You did the whole thing that fast?" he said. "It's wonderful! And this is your first painting. It is very impressive."

"Acrylics are really something," Dennis replied. "No fooling around, and they dry fast. A lot better than oils when you are in a hurry."

"When did you ever use oils?"

"Well— What I meant was that it seemed that way. I had watched people using them back in class."

"I see. You continue to amaze me. What are you doing now?"

"Learning things. I have a lot of catching up to do."

"Maybe you ought to take it a bit easy at first."

"No problem. I am not tired yet."

"Care to take another walk?"

"To tell you the truth, I would rather stay here and keep working."

"I meant to ask you about reading. . . ."

"I seem to have absorbed the basics somewhere along the line. I am working on expanding things now."

"Well, that is just great. What about dinner? You have to eat. The cafeteria is open."

"That is true. All right."

He turned off the viewer and rose, stretched.

101

"On the way over, you can tell me what things are like back on Earth," he said, "and tell me about the telepaths."

Dennis let him out, listening.

That evening, Alec made a full report to Dr. Chalmers.

". . . And I got through to him at dinnertime," he said. "He agrees that he is Dennis Guise, but he does not really believe it. He says it for our benefit. He is personally convinced that he is Leonardo da Vinci."

Dr. Chalmers snorted.

"Are you being serious?"

"Of course."

Dr. Chalmers relit his pipe.

"I don't see any harm in it," he finally said. "I do see possible harm in trying to rid him of such a delusion at this point, when it is allowing him to make such fine progress."

"I agree on leaving the da Vinci aspect alone," Alec said. "But my concern with it goes far deeper. I am not at all certain that it is a delusion."

"What do you mean?"

"I got through to him at dinnertime. He was relaxed, his thoughts drifting. I tried a probe and succeeded. He believes he is da Vinci, does not want us to know it, is doing everything he can to make us believe he is a recovering Dennis Guise. At the same time, he is trying to learn everything he can about the world in which he now finds himself."

"That does not make it anything more than a paranoid situation—one which we are fortunately able to capitalize on."

Alec raised his hand.

"It seems more than just the belief, though. With Condorcet, he picked up the man's thinking as well as the French language. Now, with da Vinci, he has acquired artistic skills, and he shifted hands—da Vinci was left-handed, I just looked it up—and an almost pathological curiosity with respect to just about everything—"

"Then why isn't he speaking Italian?"

"Because this time he has taken his thought patterns from one of the greatest minds that ever existed, and he has decided to play along with us, to fit himself into the situation in which he finds himself. He has therefore been learning modern English all day, at a phenomenal rate. If you listen to him, though, you will hear that he speaks it with an Italian accent, which he is already attempting to cover. He is trying to adapt himself."

"The entire notion is preposterous. But even granting it for a moment, by what possible mechanism could he be achieving it?"

"All right. I have been doing a lot of thinking. How does telepathy work? We are still not certain. Our approach has been mainly practical. All of our telepathic security guards, communication specialists, psychological therapy workers, semantic engineers, precision translators, have worked out various ways of exploiting the faculty without really advancing our understanding as to its mechanism. Oh, we have our theorists, but they've really very little substance on which to base their guesses."

"So you've another guess to add to the list?"

"Yes. This is really all that it is. A guess—or a strange feeling. The reason Dennis was sent here in the first place was the phenomenal range of his ability. He is the most powerful telepath on record. Here, he was effectively blocked from reaching the sorts of minds for which he seemed to have an affinity—a matter of distance. He simply could not reach far enough to make the contacts he seemed to require. Now, what did that leave him?"

"He had to fall back on his own resources. He finally did so, according to plan, and he has now begun the recovery we had hoped for."

"Unless I am right about the continued personality assumption."

"Alec! Condorcet, da Vinci and anyone else he might have been play-acting—they are all dead. Surely you are not suggesting something like spiritualism?"

"No, sir. We know even less about the nature of time than we do about telepathy. I was wondering whether, frustrated in his efforts to reach across space, he has succeeded in driving his mind back through time and actually reaching those individuals whose identities he has assumed."

Dr. Chalmers sighed.

"As in paranoia," he said, "and as in those attempted age-regressions to other lives which amateur hypnotists occasionally write books about, one significant feature is that everybody wants to be important. No one identifies himself as a skid-row bum, a serf, a common laborer. It is invariably a king, a queen, a general, a great scientist, philosopher, prophet. Does that strike you as peculiar?"

"Not really. It simply strikes me as irrelevant to Dennis' case. Granting the ability to penetrate time, those are the sorts of minds to which one would be most attracted. They were certainly the most interesting. If I would reach back, they are the ones I would attempt to scan."

"All right. This is not getting us anywhere. You say you got through to him earlier, and he is indeed convinced that he is da Vinci."

"Yes."

"Whatever the source of this new identification, it is motivating him to do things he has never attempted before. It is therefore a good thing. Let him retain his delusion. We must capitalize on it as fully as possible."

"Even if he is not really Dennis Guise?"

"Look, he answers to Dennis Guise now and he acts the way he believes Dennis Guise should act. He is suddenly showing high intelligence and the beginnings of remarkable skills. If, in his heart of hearts, he chooses to believe he is Leonardo da Vinci pulling a fast one on a world of twenty-first-century clods, what difference does it make, so long as he behaves in an acceptable fashion in all other ways? We all have our pet daydreams and fun delusions. There are certain areas where therapy ceases to be therapeutic and simply becomes meddling. Leave him with his daydream. Teach the outer man to behave in an acceptable fashion in society."

"But it is more than a daydream!"

"Alec! Hands off!"

"He is my patient."

"And I am your boss, here to make sure you do a proper job. I do not see a proper job as involving your proceeding along lines dictated by so tenuous a matter as this telepathy through time notion. We must act on the basis of knowledge, not guesswork. We do possess knowledge of paranoia, and have for a long time. Some forms are quite harmless. Leave him with that part and work on the rest. You will probably notice that as he gains more experience, becomes surer of himself, that part will simply fade away."

"You do not give me much choice."

"No, I do not."

"Okay, I will do as you say."

". . . And keep me posted, informally as well as through channels."

Alec nodded, turned to go.

"One thing more . . ." Dr. Chalmers said.

"Yes?"

"I would appreciate your keeping that notion about time to yourself, at least for now."

"Why?"

"Supposing there is something to it? Just supposing, of course. It would take a lot of substantiation, a lot of research. Premature publicity would be the worst thing."

"I understand."

"Good."

Alec went out, returned to his own quarters, stretched out on his bed to think. After a time, he slept.

The following day, Alec decided to leave Dennis alone with his studies and his painting, dropping by only at mealtimes. Dennis was not particularly communicative at breakfast or at lunch. Over dinner, however, he grew more animated, leaning forward, fixing him with his gaze.

"This—telepathic ability," he began. "It is a strange and wondrous thing."

"I thought that you said you were not going to fool with it for a while."

"That was yesterday. I said that I would not experiment with it for a time. Very well. Time has passed. I grew curious."

Alec made a small noise with his lips and shook his head.

"You could be making a serious mistake . . ." he began.

"As it turned out, I was not. I can control it. It is amazing. I have learned so many things, so quickly, by taking them from other minds."

"Whose minds?" Alec asked.

Dennis smiled.

"I do not know that it is proper to say. From yours, for instance, I learned that there is a certain code of courtesy which precludes wanton browsing among the thoughts of others."

"I see that it impressed you a lot."

Dennis shrugged.

"It works both ways. If it does not apply to me, why should I observe it myself?"

"You already know the answer to that. Your status here is that of a patient. I am your therapist. It is a special situation."

"Then I do not see why I should be castigated for my actions by those who do not consider me fully responsible for them."

Alec chuckled.

"Very good," he said. "You are learning fast. Obviously, things should be revised very soon. In the meantime, all I can say is that it is just not nice."

Dennis nodded.

"No argument there. I have better uses for my time than voyeurism. No. I was leading up to a discussion of two things in which I am currently interested: my own case, and the telepathic function itself."

"If you have indeed been behaving as you indicated, then you probably know as much about them both as we do."

"Hardly," he said. "I cannot plumb the depths of your mind and dredge up all your experience and skill."

"Oh? Since when? You seemed able to manage it before."

"When?"

"Let me ask you a question first. Do you remember anything of other periods of clarity, times when you felt as if you were someone else?"

"I—I do not think so. Things—like dreams—sometimes come and go, though. Idle thoughts, occasional disjointed fragments of something like memory. But I do not really have much to associate with them. Do you mean that I *have* been other people, that everything I now feel and think is just some sort of—overlay? Are you saying that there is really someone else buried within me and that the person I think I am may be subject to recall at any time?"

"No, I am not saying that."

"What, then?"

"I do not know, Dennis. You know yourself better than I do. You appear to be learning things at a fantastic pace—"

"You do not believe that I am really Dennis Guise," he said.

"Are you?"

"That is a silly question."

"You raised it."

"You think that I am still some sort of overlay, and that the real Dennis Guise is still buried within me?"

"Dennis, I do not know. You are my patient. More than anything else, I want to see you fully recovered and functioning normally in society. It was never my intention to raise these doubts in your mind. A therapist just naturally tends to speculate, to go over every possibility, no matter how farfetched. Generally, these things remain unvoiced. At this point, it seems unfortunate that you are such a good telepath and that you chose to exercise your ability just when you did."

"Then you are saying that you now feel you were wrong in this?"

"I am saying it was just one of those guesses one sometimes makes with very little to go on. Guesses are made and discarded countless times during a course of therapy. It should not really concern you."

Dennis took a drink of juice.

"But it does, you know," he said, after a time. "I am not tremendously fond of the notion that I am keeping the rightful inhabitant of this body, this brain, from his proper existence."

"Even if he may never be so fit as yourself to do so?"

"Even so."

"Beyond the fact that this is all idle speculation, I fail to see where there is much that you can do about your tenancy."

"I suppose you are right. It is an interesting hypothetical situation, however, and coming out of the dark as I so recently have, matters of an existential nature do hold a certain fascination."

"I can see that. However, I feel that this is not the best time to consider them—coming out of the dark as you so recently have, as you put it."

"I can see why a therapist would feel that way. . . . But I may be more stable than you realize."

"Then why are you expressing all these doubts about yourself? No. I want to give you support right now, not provide a dissection of your inner landscape. Let all this pass, will you? Concentrate on perfecting your strengths. After more time has passed, these problems may not seem as important as they do now."

"I have a feeling that you are talking for Dr. Chalmers rather than yourself."

"Then consider the idea, not its source. You were ill, you are getting better. These are two things we know, two things we have to work with. The hell with theory. The hell with speculation. Curb your introspective tendencies for the time being and concentrate on matters of substance."

"Easily said. But all right, let us drop it."

"Good. You realize that it is the next thing to miraculous that we are speaking of things at this level this soon? You are an amazing person. If this is any indication of what you are to become we should both be impressed."

"Yes, I guess that you are right. I should be thankful for this flash of existence which has been granted me. Now, just for purposes of rounding out my education, tell me about this telepathy through time business that I caught a thought or two concerning, here and there. Is there anything at all on it in the literature?"

"No. I have checked recently. There is not."

"Have you ever managed it yourself?"

"No."

"Any idea how it might be done?"

"None whatsoever."

"Pity, is it not—when you consider all the things that might be learned from the past, if it could be taken more seriously?"

"One day . . . Who knows?"

"Indeed," he said, and he rose from the table.

Alec stood also.

"Walk you back?" he asked.

"Thank you, but I would rather be alone. There are many things I wish to think about."

"All right. Sure. You know where my rooms are, if you should want to talk about anything—any time."

"Yes. Thanks again."

Alec watched him go, seated himself and finished his coffee.

The next day, Dennis did not take breakfast with Alec, nor did he invite him into his room. Through the partly opened door, he told him that he was very busy and was going to skip that meal. He offered no comment on the nature of his activities. After breakfast, Alec checked the tape in the monitor for Dennis' room, from which he learned that the light had been burning all night and that Dennis had alternated between long periods at his easel and sitting motionless in his armchair.

Returning at lunchtime, Alec received no answer when he knocked on the door. He called out several times, but there was no response to this either. Finally, he opened the door and entered.

Dennis lay on the bed, clutching at his side. His eyes were fixed on the ceiling and a small trickle of saliva had run back over his cheek.

Alec moved to his side.

"Dennis! What is it?" he asked. "What happened?"

"I—" he said. "I—" and his eyes filled with tears.

"I'll get you a doctor," Alec said.

"I am—" Dennis said, and his face relaxed, his hands fell away from his side.

As Alec turned to go, his eyes fell upon the canvas still resting on the easel and he stood for several moments, staring.

It bore a study of the Mona Lisa, quite complete and exquisitely rendered, he thought, because acrylics are so much better than oils. That has to be it, he thought. I remember that that was his thought, right before he hurried out.

Part IV

I am.

I remember them all. There were so many. But I do not remember myself, because I was not there. Not before that moment.

It was in that moment that I first knew myself.

That moment.

Once there was a man. His name was Gilbert Van Duyn. We watched him in the General Assembly of the United Nations. Watched him get up to say that the preservation of the Earth required some sacrifice. Watched as the world froze about him. Watched him make his way through that still landscape of flesh. Watched him go out of the hall and meet the dark man. Watched them fly to the roof of the tower and regard the city, the world. Listened to the dark man's story. Watched them return to the ground. Watched Gilbert Van Duyn return to the hall, to the lectern. Watched as there was movement once more and the bullet struck us. Watched the blue flag as the life left us, by our own choice.

And in that moment we knew, I knew.

Once there was a man. And so I am.

He who showed me these things claimed that nothing was ever done. He died at that moment also, again, that I might live. Yet he lives in me still. A man there once was.

And I fled through all I had ever been, over that bridge of ashes, the past. To each, each, as he died or was conquered. And I was there. There were men. And I am so.

Fled that final image that gave me birth, each to

each to each, and it returned, ever, to the final sight of Gilbert Van Duyn's eyes, the first sight of my own. I. I fled.

Back, back to the place where the dark man lay bleeding. Dying? Dying also, like the others? But he lived, and rose, and moved again among his children. I saw through his eyes, and I knew. Once a man there was. And a woman. And I knew. I began to understand.

All, all, all of them came clear to me now. The hundreds I had known. Or was it more? There is no count. All. I knelt atop the building and raised the .30/06, sighting in on the governor. Fallen, I watched my blood pool as the Persian army pressed the attack. There, in the sand, I strove to create the calculus, when the sword came into me. And you, my Thérèse! Where are you tonight? My words have been eaten by the wind. My vision doubles in my head and the world is twice as monstrous. I squeeze the trigger and the man falls before thunder. I shift the barrel. Here in my cell, I contemplate the Terror and think upon the future of man. My own end will be small by comparison. I sketch the elements, here at Amboise, the great forces that walk naked in the air and on the seas, the high storms with their winds, the rushing of mighty waves. I shoot again and another man falls. I wipe the .30/06 quickly but carefully, as planned, lean it against the wall beside the mark of the Children of the Earth, turn, crouching, and begin my retreat along the rooftops. There, atop the building, I follow the dark man's gesture and regard the East River, a piece of muddy glass, and the hazed and grainy sky where strands of smoke lay like bloated things on a beach. Then to the other side, where I look upon the tangled city. Driving, driving through the night, a pain in my shoulder and hoping for rain. But the land lay still and rugged. So be it. I may prefer it another way, yet still it pleases me that the grasses are dry and the animals in their burrows. The pleasure and the pride of humanity are best enjoyed against the heedlessness, the slumbering power of the Earth. Even when it moves to crush, it adds something. To isolate oneself too much from it detracts from both our achievements and our failures. We must feel the forces we live with. . . .

And the white circle on the field of blue remains for a moment as all else collapses about me. Then it, too, fades and is gone. Only I remain, a rock fresh-exposed above the beat of the surf. I am Dennis Guise.

Alec has left the room, is hurrying to fetch a doctor. The pain lessens in my side as I understand.

Alec's recent thoughts echo within me and I turn my head to regard the acrylics which dry so fast, seeing there on the easel the lady he has left me, smiling.

Once there was a man.

I ran a fever. I know that I was delirious. I slept a lot. I was in and out of the fog countless times during the next couple of days. As things finally settled, I became aware once again of the dispensary ceiling and of Alec's gentle presence at my side.

"Got any water there?" I asked him.

"Just a minute," he said, and I heard him pour it. "Here you are."

He passed me a glass with a bent straw in it. I held it with both hands and drank.

"Thanks," I said, passing it back.

"How are you—feeling?"

I managed a chuckle. I could feel his mental probing. Better not to block it entirely at this point, or to let him know that I was blocking at all—or that I was even aware of his quick survey.

"I am—myself," I said. "Ask me my name, if you wish."

"Never mind. I would give a lot to understand all the preliminaries—to this."

"Me, too. I am weak. I feel well, though."

"What do you remember of the events of the past two months?"

"Not much. Fragments. Disconnected impressions."

"You *are* a new person."

"Glad to hear you say it. I think so, too."

"Well, I have a feeling that you have just taken a major step toward recovery."

"I could use another drink."

He refilled the glass and I emptied it. I covered my mouth and yawned after I had passed it back to him.

"You seem to be right-handed."

"So I do. I am sorry, but I think that I am going back to sleep again."

"Sure. Rest easy. I will be around. You should be up and out of here in no time now, unless my guess is way off."

I nodded and let my eyelids droop.

"Good," I said. "Glad to hear it."

I closed my eyes and let my mind swim. Alec rose and departed.

I knew, even then, what I had to do, and I was scared. I had to find one man, out of the entire population of the Earth, and ask him how to go about it. Which meant that I had to convince the staff here of my cure—I suppose that is a better word than "recovery," since I had never been normal—and of my continuing stability in order to be permitted to return to Earth. Which meant I must work to assure this condition. Time was essential, or so it seemed to me then. I hoped that I had not happened too late.

I was not at all clear as to the particulars of what it was that separated me from the others I had known and been. It seemed worth seeking the information just then, especially since there was not much else I could do at the moment. With a full medical staff about, it was just a matter of locating the proper person.

I moved forth with my mind, searching.

Shortly, I found that person, a woman working in the lab two buildings over, a molecular biologist, a Dr. Holmes. The thoughts were not right there at the surface, but there were indications that she had the concepts on file. I sought more deeply.

Yes. J. B. S. Haldane had once calculated that the deaths resulting from the operation of natural selection in the substitution of a new model gene for an old one were so great that the species could only afford the es-

116

tablishment of a new gene every millennium or so. This view had held sway for a long while, but then a new notion of mutationism arose in 1968. The rapid growth of molecular biology around that time had had a lot to do with it. In the February issue of that year's *Nature* there had appeared a paper by the geneticist Motoo Kimura, wherein he speculated over the great differences then recently determined to exist among the hemoglobin, cytochrome c and other molecules in various species of animals. They were much commoner than had previously been supposed. Considering the large number of molecules and genes, it would seem that a mutation must be established every few years. He felt that such a high rate of molecular evolution was only feasible if most of them were neither helpful nor harmful, representing random, neutral mutations drifting through populations. This raised hell among classical evolutionaries because it indicated that evolution might be influenced by a strong element of random genetic drift, in other words a much higher chance factor, than good old natural selection. The new techniques, put to work in earnest on seeking molecular alternatives in living populations, continued to uncover them in abundance—gratuitous changes, giving rise to molecular diversity. . . .

Which meant . . .

Which meant that the sleeping masters of human evolution, of whom the dark man had informed Van Duyn, could not possibly have a *complete* say in the development of the species. They would have had more control long ago, with a smaller population, in determining the route we would take. Once established as man, however, once spread across the entire globe and breeding our way through the hundreds of millions and finally the billions, there was no way to continue this control by means of whatever primary influences they had once exercised. Nor was this necessary, since we were proceeding in the proper direction. Once we were established as a rational, toolmaking crowd, their task shifted over to one of superintendancy, to keeping a watchful eye or three on our ideas, philosophies, technological developments, pruning the undesired and encouraging its opposite. This was all that they could do, once we had passed some numerical milestones. They could not fully predict nor control the random genetic developments which must arise with statistically greater frequency with the increasing population. It was no special response in terms of natural selection for mankind to have come up with the TP gene, but we had. There was no obvious threat in it, and the sleepers had not moved against us. Now, though, I existed. I understood the situation, I had access to the past experience of the race. . . .

And I was scared, for I would now have to get a clean bill of health and go looking for the man. . . .

And I was tired. Even thinking about it was going to have to wait a little longer. . . .

In the weeks and months that followed, I learned. I attended classes, I followed programmed courses of study, I listened to tapes and watched viewscreens, I talked with Alec and let him see what I wished him to see in my mind. I participated in group therapy sessions, I exercised my special talent to learn of more things. I waited.

During this time, I felt the easing of tension about me, and I came to regard Alec more as a friend than a therapist. We talked about a great variety of subjects, played games together in the gym. A later scan of Dr. Chalmers' thinking equipment even showed me that Alec had broached the subject of my return to Earth somewhat ahead of schedule.

"You really ought to be doing more calisthenics," Alec had said. "Knee bends with weights would be useful."

"Sounds awful," I replied.

"Can't let yourself waste away," he said. "Supposing they recommended a trial visit down yonder and you were in no shape to go?"

"Are they thinking about it?"

"I couldn't say. But if they were to, would you want to hang back for a month or so, just because you had not been paying attention to the physical prelimi-naries?"

"Now that you mention it," I said, "no. But the whole idea raises a matter I have not really spent any time thinking about."

"What is that?"

"My parents. I have already gathered that their sep-aration is probably a permanent thing. When the time does come for me to go back, where do I go?"

Alec moistened his lips and looked away.

"Do not worry about all that anxiety business," I said. "It is a pretty neutral matter to me after all the sessions I have had with Dr. McGinley. I just want to know where I go when I do go."

"Dennis, the matter has not really been discussed yet. I do not know whether your parents will fight over your custody. Do you have a preference?"

"As I said, I have not really given the matter much thought. Would my choice count for much?"

"From all reports I have received, your parents are both reasonable people. They have been very pleased with your progress here. They both want to see you again. You have had letters from both of them. Was there anything in them that might influence your pref-erence?"

"No."

"Then I can only suggest that you spend some time thinking about which one you would rather be with. There is still plenty of time. When the day does come that you have to make a choice, I can add a suggestion that it would be best for your adjustment to honor your preference—for whatever that may be worth."

"Thanks, Alec. Show me some of the exercises I should be doing, huh?"

... And this was what caused me to go rummaging in Dr. Chalmers' head. I had found myself loathe to probe Alec since we had become friends.

Later, I thought about the matters he had raised. My father had money, power, connections—all of which could be useful in my quest—and he was now living in Washington, near to so many other things and places which might benefit me in the search. My mother was still in northern New Mexico, tending her flowers, isolated. But my father would not have much time for me—a good thing, if that was all there would be to it. Only, with full access to my own impressions past, I could now form a picture of the man. It was my guess that he would enroll me in a fancy private school, someplace where they would make a fuss about nonattendance, would keep a tight rein on me. On the other hand, I was certain that I could persuade my mother to let me stay at home, coming and going pretty much as I chose, continuing my education in programmed units via a rented machine similar to the one I was using here. At least, I would have a better chance of working things that way with her than I would with him.

Then I asked myself another: Aside from these considerations, if everything else were simple and uncomplicated, who would I really want to go to?

I could not make up my mind. I almost welcomed the external factors, terrible as they were, which relieved me of the necessity of making a real choice.

And so I prepared myself, physically and mentally, for my return. A month later, the matter was mentioned officially. Dr. Chalmers came around to see me, commended my progress, told me he felt that perhaps another month of preparation and observation was in order and if everything continued as was expected I could go home and see how things worked out. It was then that he asked me which home I might prefer. Keeping in tune with the therapeutic note I had sounded, I told him that I felt the simpler the environment the more comfortable I might feel. He seemed to think that was a good choice, and I saw in his mind that I would have his recommendation, also.

Which is how things worked out. I was given a provisionally clean bill the following month and a date was set. I realized during that time that I was growing increasingly anxious, not so much over the task I had set myself, but simply at the thought of heading for that place in the sky, so full of people and things. I visited the observation deck on numerous occasions, assumed my old chair and watched the world, glowing, mysterious, attracting and frightening by turns, far and yet near. I fancied a summons, I assumed a threat.

Despite the exposure involved in all my vicarious existences and the sum of my salvaged personal impressions, I had never been there before, as a rational, individual being. I talked about it with Alec and he told me that it was a natural feeling, a thing to be expected, a thing that would vanish not too long after I got back. I had already thought these thoughts myself, but as with so many other conclusions, it was nevertheless comforting to hear them from another.

In my room, I paced, stared at the paintings, paced some more, thumbed through the sketches, again and again. The lady smiled.

Finally, I packed them all carefully and went to sit by the fountain. I walked among the flowerbeds.

I began taking all my meals in the cafeteria, and for the first time I began talking with the other patients. There was one old man whose eyes misted over when he learned that I was going back.

"Go to New Jersey," he said.

"New Jersey?"

"Not the cities. The pinelands. They still stand as they did when I was a boy. Go there one day and look at the trees. Get out and walk among them. If you ever do that, think of me then," he said. "Promise."

He reached out and laid a hand on my arm, veins like blue worms crawling across the back of his hand. He leaned forward and his breath was bad.

"Promise."

I nodded. I could not speak, for his tremor, his faded eyes, his odor, were lost in the barrage of thoughts that fell upon me: cranberries, huckleberries, blueberries, sweet fern, sheep laurel, dewy mornings, sunshot days, foggy evenings, bogs, the smell of pine, a gentle rainfall, autumn smoke, winter's chill, homemade whisky ... Pieces, textures ... Memories. His vanished youth. A place to which he literally could not go home. With difficulty, I raised a shield against these things.

"I will remember," I said finally; and thereafter I maintained a tight shield when speaking with my fellow patients.

When the time came, most of the staff and some of the patients turned out to see me off. I said my good-byes, to Alec, to Dr. Chalmers, to the others, then boarded the monorail that was to take me to Luna Station. I tried to hide my emotions with a forced casualness, not wanting them to think I was anything less than stable at this point. However, my voice broke and I embraced Alec before I boarded. This was, after all, the only real home I had known, as myself, Dennis Guise. I paid little heed to the rocks, the craters, the inky shadows I raced past. I thought only of what I was leaving and where I was going.

I was landed at the field in Texas, and my mother met me there. My first impressions of Earth were mainly of the countless thoughts which swirled about. It was easy to see how they had unbalanced me as a child. Now, though, I was able to put them aside, ignore them, force them into the background, turn them off.

"Dennis . . ." she said, and there were tears in her eyes. She kissed me. "You—you understand things now?"

"Yes," I said. "I'm all right."

. . . And all this does not bother you?

There was an initial shock. It has already passed. I can handle the thoughts now.

You will never know what it was like.

I remember some things.

It is so good to see you well, to finally know you. . . .

I nodded and tried to smile.

We are going home now. Come this way.

She took my arm and led me from the terminal.

How to begin?

It was strange, settling into my old room. I had

memories of the place, but it was almost as if they belonged to someone else, a phenomenon with which I was not entirely unfamiliar. I spent days of introspection, sifting through my old recollections of the place. This was less an exercise in morbidity than a search for things of value.

The teaching machine arrived and was installed. My father was footing the bill for it. I spoke with him on a number of occasions. He wanted me to come see him as soon as I felt able. He promised to come see me as soon as he could get away. I began using the machine.

Established now, with some of my feelings and thoughts sorted out, I commenced the efforts I had been contemplating since my arousal in the dispensary on Luna.

Each day, I undertook a telepathic search, swinging and skimming about the world, seeking one mind or some sign of its existence. The act was not as hopeless as it sounds, for I was certain that the one I sought would stand out like a beacon on a dark night. Even as the days passed without the slightest intimation of his existence, I did not grow discouraged. The world is a large place. I was learning things, I was refining my skills.

But the weeks passed and there was nothing. It had of course occurred to me that the man I sought might well be dead. It had been a long time since his last appearance. His enemies might finally have caught up with him. I redoubled my efforts. I could do nothing but keep looking.

It was on a Friday evening that I came across something peculiar. I had climbed a nearby hill, a concession to my mother's complaint that I was not getting enough exercise, and seated on a rock out of sight of the house I had set forth with my mind once again, casting first at places nearer to home. After a quarter of an hour of wandering, I encountered familiar thought-patterns. When I closed with them, I determined that they originated in Albuquerque, and I became aware of the thinker's plans for the following day. He would be heading north, and passing on the highway, not too far to the east. I was filled with excitement. He was not my quarry, but he was someone I greatly desired to meet.

When I returned to the house, my mother saw my face, felt my mood and smiled.

"I told you," she said. "Exercise. This is the best I've seen you look."

"Yes, Mother," I said.

"You will be in good condition for your surprise tomorrow."

"Surprise? What is it?"

"If I told you . . ." she began.

"It isn't Dad, is it? Is he coming?"

She looked away.

"No," she said, "not your father. You will just have to wait and see."

I thought of trying a probe, but she would have caught it and blocked it, I am certain. And she wanted it to be a surprise. I left it at that. I had more important matters to consider, anyhow.

I yawned.

"All this fresh air and altitude . . . I am going to turn in early."

"Good idea," she said, and kissed me.

I was up early the next morning. Before I even got out of bed, I reached out with my mind and found my man. Then I left a note saying that I had gone for a walk, and I made my way to a bluff above the highway. I seated myself and waited, listening to his thoughts as he drove on.

After a long while, the car came into view. I climbed down and waited at the side of the road.

When the vehicle drew near, I stepped out into the road and raised my hands. I was in his mind at the time and saw that he had noticed me and was going to stop. Else I would have gotten out of the way.

He braked to a halt and called out, "What's the matter, kid?"

I walked up beside the machine, studying the face of the man I had once been.

"Hello, Quick," I said. "It's been a while."

He stared at me, then shook his head.

"I'm sorry, he said. "I don't remember where . . ."

"I remember the shootout when they got Leishman," I said. "You got the last cop and made it away. They never did figure out who the other man was."

His eyes widened, then narrowed.

"Who the hell are you, anyway?"

"I have to talk with you. It's important."

"All right. Get in," he said.

"No, thanks. Why don't you pull off to the side and get out? We can climb up in those rocks across the way."

"Why?"

"It's a place to sit down."

"Is anyone else there?"

"No."

He pulled over, opened the door and stepped out.

"I want you to know something—" he began.

"—that you are carrying a loaded .32 automatic in the right-hand pocket of your jacket," I said, "and you intend to shoot anyone else you encounter the moment you see him. But I am not lying to you. There is no one else. I just want to talk."

"How did you—? Are you a telepath?"

"Yes."

"Okay. Anyplace special?"

"No. Just up."

"Lead on."

He followed me to the top, found himself a perch and lit a cigarette.

"What do you want?" he asked.

"First," I said, "I wanted to meet you. You see, once I was you."

"Come again?"

"I will have to tell you something about myself . . ." I began. And I did. I told him of my condition, of how I had become Leishman and been used to trace him, of how I had later, briefly, been Quick Smith. The sun was higher when I finished.

He had remained silent as I had spoken, nodding occasionally. Now he sat, staring off toward the horizon, as if listening to some faraway voice. I waited for him to say something, but he did not.

I cleared my throat.

"That is—my story," I said, finally. "I wanted you to know that much before—"

"Yes, it is—quite interesting," he said then. "You certainly are a different sort of person. Now what?"

"Now? Now I was going to ask you, as the only COE member handy, whether you really believe that our rural past possessed all the virtues, whether all the clichés about cities might not make that past seem like something it never was, whether exploitation of the land and the people—like child labor—might not have been far worse in the old days, as it still is in agrarian countries today, whether the cities might not really offer more than they have taken when contrasted with that past."

"That was not what I meant when I said 'Now what?' and that is a string of loaded questions," he said. "But I will give you an answer anyway, before I go back to it. I am hardly a spokesman for the COE. I am just a dirtywork specialist. It is true that a lot of us might romanticize the simpler life, turn it into a pastoral. I am not one of them. I grew up on a farm. I was child labor myself. I do not have it in for the cities. In fact, they represented something I wanted to get away to as soon as I could swing it. They may well offer more than they have taken. I think that they probably do. I am just a dirty, mean little guy who was probably simply a troublemaker to begin with. If it had not been the COE it would have been something else—then. Your asking me these things makes me think back over it, though. Now, it is a bit different. But okay . . . For all that, when I look back at my childhood, I see that I always loved the land. I can't romanticize it, I was too close to it. I am a conservationist, an environmentalist, an ecological activist—whatever term is currently fashionable—because I am pro-land, not anti-city. You set up a false dichotomy when you reeled off those questions. Being for the land does not mean being against the city. We cannot junk them all and turn back the clock. Not now. When we blow up a dam or screw up a source of pollution, we are not telling them to turn off all the technology in the world. We are telling them to be more judicious in its disposition, we are encouraging the consideration, the development, of alternatives. There are men who see no more in public lands than lumber, minerals, grazing and the building of dams, men who claim they are benefiting the people in this and are really only out for a fast buck. Rod told me the history of the national parks, for example. They faced this kind of invasion and destruction, with the same excuses offered, long before our present problems existed. I want to protect what remains of the natural world, that's all. Now you tell me something. I had asked you, 'Now what?' What I meant was, you have this powerful ability no other telepath seems to have developed yet. What are you going to do with it?"

"What do you mean?"

"Your interest in these matters seems more than simple curiosity. I could not help but wonder—"

His eyes flicked upward, past my shoulder.

I had not heard anyone approach, nor felt them with my mind, and I was not in Quick's mind at the moment. I turned.

She had come up the easy grade on the far side of the bluff. She seemed taller than I remembered, and a trifle thinner.

"Lydia!" I said, rising. "Mother spoke of a surprise. . . ."

She smiled.

"Hello, Dennis," she said. "Hello, Quick."

"You know each other?" I asked.

Quick nodded.

"Oh yes," he said. "We've met. A long time ago. How've you been?"

"Fine," she said, drawing nearer.

"Lydia is the therapist I mentioned," I said, "who took care of me. Before."

"Quick, you have changed," she said.

He nodded.

"Everyone does, I guess," he said.

She looked at me again.

Dennis, let me see you.

I nodded and felt her move further into my mind.

After a time, *Congratulations. We have succeeded,* she told me. *You exist. You have followed the leads that I left you. You are seeking . . . What?*

A man. The man who spoke with Van Duyn, years back.

Why?

To ask how I can help him with his efforts.

What makes you feel you have anything to offer?

You know that I am special.

You feel that is enough—being special?

I guess that is for him to decide.

It is good that you wish to help. Supposing he asked of you what he asked of Van Duyn?

I do not know. It would be a waste.

Perhaps. Whatever, I will help you in your search. So will this man.

How?

Later, Dennis. Later. All in good time. We had best get to your home now.

"You are heading north, Quick?" she asked.

"Denver, to spend a few days with some friends."

"Let me know where I can get in touch with you, all right? There is an enterprise in which you may be useful."

"Sure," he said, and he fished a piece of paper from his pocket, scrawled something on it, passed it to her. "I'll be at the first one till Tuesday, the next one afterward."

"Very good. Thank you. You may hear from me before too long. Have a nice trip."

"Thanks. So long."

"Goodbye."

He headed back down toward the road. We went the other way.

We walked back to where Lydia's car was parked on a side road. From there we drove on home, announcing that Lydia had encountered me on my morning hike. My mother prepared breakfast, and the morning was spent in conversation. After lunch, Lydia examined me at some length. I tried blocking in some areas, just to see what the result would be. She caught me on all of them.

Excellent, she told me after a long while. *You have exceeded my expectations.*

In what way?

I mean that you have pulled through beautifully.

That is not what you mean. You are masking something.

You are *good. Congratulations.*

That is not an answer.

Let us say then that it was really a form of directive therapy in which we engaged.

There was not really that much of me to direct.

I did not say that it was easy.

Did you influence the development of my temporopathic ability?

No, but I might have influenced the kinds of choices you would make if you did succeed in reaching back after other minds in times gone by.

Why?

I only said "might."

You did not come back just to play games with me, did you?

No. You will have your answers in good time.

Where does Quick figure in all this?

He did some work for me once.

Is there anything at all that you feel like telling me?

Yes, but you are not letting me. You are asking all the wrong questions.

What are the right ones?

I said that I would help you in your search. You said that you want to find the dark man. Had you asked me, I could have told you that he is still living. Had you asked me where, I could have told you that you will find him in East Africa.

You know him?

Yes, I know him.

I have searched, but I found no trace. . . .

You will not find him unless he chooses to be found.

Why is this?

His is a cautious way of life.

Yes, I gathered that they seek him in particular.

They may seek you now, also.

Why?

You have been broadcasting your presence ever since your return. They are suspicious of concentrations of power in the hands of a single individual. They must convince themselves it is harmless, tame it, turn it or destroy it.

Then I am in danger, even now?

It is possible. This is the reason I came so soon. You are firm in your decision?

I am.

Then we must leave as soon as possible. The longer we delay the less your chance of reaching your goal. They have human agents as well as mechanical devices.

Are the enemies TP, also?

That, or something like it. They have their ways of knowing things.

How shall we go about the whole business?

I have already obtained travel papers in your name. This evening we shall discuss with you mother your desire to see more of the world now that you are adjusted to this much of it. I will second the idea as a therapeutically sound thing. I believe that I can persuade her.

Supposing she wants to come along?

This possibility has been considered. Fortunately, her contacts with your father since your return seem to be leading them toward a reconciliation. I believe they are going to discuss the matter this evening. Should this come to pass, they might well appreciate your absence on a short trip.

How can you know all these things?

As a TP and a personal friend—

No! That is too much to ask me to believe.

What, then, would you believe?

The only alternative that presents itself. You are

130

devious, Lydia. I know that now, from my own case, from your plans for handling these things, from your acquaintanceship with a COE troubleshooter. I am forced to entertain the possibility that you possess considerable means for manipulating people and situations, that you are somehow responsible for my parents' breakup and their coming reconciliation, for my transfer to the moon—for the entire course my condition has taken. I suddenly look upon you as the architect of my existence.

Ridiculous!

Call it whatever you want. That is how I feel about it.

Then believe whatever you want. Does it affect your plans?

No. I am still going. I have to.

Good. Then the rest does not matter.

But it does. You see, I am not going to forget. If I live a few more years I am going to be even stronger than I am now. If I ever discover that you caused my parents needless pain, I want you to know that I am not going to forget.

She lowered her head.

So be it then.

And things worked out pretty much as Lydia had said. Dad called and wanted to come out. To see me, he said. Mother said okay, and he arrived the next day. I quickly saw that Lydia had been right. They hit things off and were talking friendly again right from the start. He was happy enough to see me, very happy. We had several long talks and even went walking together a few times. But it was plain that he had come back for more than that.

It began to occur to me about then that perhaps I had been too hard on Lydia. Common decency forbade my trying to probe my parents' thoughts at that time, but I suddenly realized that the strain of my prolonged condition must have been pretty hard on them, particularly on Dad. I may well have contributed to the initial breakup, just as my recovery might have served as catalyst to the reconciliation. It had been insensitive of me not to have realized this earlier. It began to seem possible that, though I still felt Lydia to be a manipulator, she had in this one respect merely capitalized on something already present, rather than creating the entire situation. It left her no less culpable, if she had somehow provided the necessary pushes at various points, but it softened the picture somewhat, if only through the mitigating agency of my own newfound guilt feelings.

And these feelings made me anxious to be under way, as anxious perhaps as my parents were for some time alone together. At least, they bought Lydia's endorsement of my request for a vacation, seeing that I would be accompanied by herself and a male nurse of her acquaintance.

"It's good to have you back, son."

It did not seem so ironic later that these were the last words my father said to me as Lydia and I boarded the flier that was to take us to Albuquerque. After the talks we had had I came to realize that my recovery was a source of pride to him—the fact that I had made it through a rough piece of existence— possibly even greater than his pleasure in knowing that my ability transcended any other on record. Mine was a sadder feeling than I had thought it would be, at another leave-taking this soon after my return. I waved to them as we rose and did not let down my shield till we reached the town.

The flight out of Albuquerque was uneventful. Lydia had warned me of the possibility of danger from that point on. But I scanned all my fellow passengers and found nothing alarming. In fact, it grew boring after a time, and I read most of the way to Libreville, in Gabon. Only Quick seemed constantly alert.

Shortly after our arrival, a man appeared at our hotel with a case full of pistols. Quick selected one—a revolver—and a box of cartridges. No money changed hands. Lydia shielded the man's mind, but I was still able to skim a few surface thoughts indicating his connection with a local COE-type group.

"With this," Lydia said to Quick, "you are in a position to take over my function as bodyguard. I have to go on ahead now to make arrangements, which gives you a little time to spend." She passed him a slip of paper. "Be at this field in Moanda at 1800 hours, tomorrow. You will be met there and transported east."

It was not clear to me how she could have been acting as a bodyguard, but then Quick had never seemed much like a male nurse either. I refrained from commenting.

"What is there to do in this town?" Quick asked her.

"For one thing, you can get out of it in a hurry," she replied, smiling. "There are more instructions on the back of the page. Take the shuttle down to Moanda tonight and go visit that place tomorrow."

Quick turned the sheet, read there, looked up.

"What do we do when we get there?"

"Sightsee. That is all. Look at that thing and think about it. Nothing more. An amusement perhaps. A way of passing the time."

"All right. Shall we get something to eat now?"

"Let's."

Lydia departed after dinner, and Quick and I returned to the hotel and checked out. We caught the shuttle and leaned back to watch the country pass. After a time, I dozed and did not awaken until we had reached our destination. It was quite late when we checked into the local hostel, and we turned in immediately.

I was awakened.

I had come around suddenly from a very deep sleep, a strong feeling of pursuit filling my mind. For several moments, I was Leishman again, wondering at the enemy's identity, assessing the unfamiliar surroundings, dim in the darkened room. Then I knew a sense of wrongness. This was someone else's game.

Look up, old man! We must answer! The blade comes out of the scabbard. . . .

I grew with the shudder which followed, and Leishman faded to something more than memory, less than controller.

I was in a better position than Leishman to understand the situation.

Some TP was attempting to scan us. I set up a partial block, covering my main thinking, leaving a jumble of reverie for his consideration: moonlight, shadow, the texture of the bedclothes, a small thirst, bladder pressure, the various night sounds from beyond the window. Within this fortress, I was troubled that he had already had a look at the Leishman persona.

I slid out of bed, crossed to the window, stood beside it and looked out.

The night was warm and a dank breeze was blowing from the direction of an irrigation ditch we had crossed earlier. The nearest streetlight was on a corner far to my right. Carefully, with thoughts and eyes, I sought the mental eavesdropper.

I became aware of a figure in a shadowed doorway up the street.

Still blocking, I retreated, moved to Quick's bedside. I placed a hand on his shoulder.

He gave no physical sign of having come awake, but said softly, "What is it?"

I moved to cover his thoughts, also. I said, "There is a TP trying to read us. I am preventing it. He is across the street, in a doorway to the right. What should we do?"

He did not answer, but sat up, reached for his trousers, pulled them on. He stuck his feet into his boots and rose, running both hands through his hair.

"Keep preventing him," he said, drawing on his shirt and crossing to the door, buttoning it as he went. "Lock the door after me."

"The gun is still under your pillow."

"That's a good place for it."

I locked the door and followed him with my mind, holding a total shield about his thoughts. I found it easier than I thought it would be to maintain my own partial shield while doing this—slow stream of consciousness, surface thoughts leaking. I returned to my bed and lay down.

As the minutes passed, I realized that the observer was not merely observing. A gentle but definite pressure began to occur as he tried to influence my exposed train of reverie. It was something I had never attempted myself: taking control of another mind. I permitted him to gain his simple objectives, wondering the while whether I should make an effort to try the same maneuver on him.

Before I could make the decision, however, the pressure was off and the sounds of a scuffle occurred beyond the window. I dropped my shields and raced across the room. I could make out little beyond the movement of shadows within a courtyard to the left of the doorway our observer had occupied. I moved into Quick's mind and was swept up by a sequence of motor activity.

. . . We were blocking a knife thrust, then chopping with the edge of our hand. We kicked then and closed for a succession of blows. There was a brief pause, then a final, calculated chop. . . .

I broke off contact immediately. I lay quietly and attempted to still my mind.

Later, when I let Quick in, I asked him, "What did you do with the body?"

"Irrigation ditch," he said.

"I suppose it was necessary . . . ?"

"He didn't give me much choice."

"And if he had?"

"I hate hypothetical questions."

He returned to his bed, got in. I went back to mine.

"How much do you know about where we are going, what we are going to find there?" I asked him.

"Absolutely nothing. Lydia says it is important. That is enough."

"How is it that you know her?"

He coughed. Then, "I'd supposed you had found that in my mind."

"I don't go poking around in my friends' heads."

"Good to hear," he said.

135

"So how did you meet her?"

"She saved me once when I was running from the police. Came up to me on the street in Omaha, called me by name and told me I had better go with her if I wanted to be safe. So I did. She put me up for a couple of days and got me out of town. She got me fake papers and a legitimate job while I was lying low. Later, I did some work for her."

"What sort of work?"

"Oh, you might say courier, guard, delivery boy."

"I don't quite follow you."

"That's all right. Go to sleep."

"Is she COE?"

He was silent for a time. Then, "I don't really know," he said. "Sometimes I think so. But I have never been certain. She is certainly sympathetic."

"I see."

"Probably not. G'night."

"'Night."

In the morning we had a bad breakfast and found transportation out to the site. I did some probing but was unable to discover any sign that a body had been found in the ditch. Perhaps it had not yet been located. Or perhaps it was a common occurrence and excited no special interest.

It took over an hour to get out to the mine and the temperature was already beginning to rise out of the comfort range when we arrived. A number of our fellow passengers proved to be part of a tour. We stayed near them to benefit from their guide's explanations.

Following, we approached an abandoned open pit mine, taking a trail that led around to its far side. We drew up beside a railed-in area. As we walked, the guide had explained that it once was a uranium mine, from which over 800 tons of the metal had been extracted annually in the late twentieth century, until it finally gave out. Most of it had gone to France.

". . . And here," he said, leaning on the rail and gesturing, "is the truly interesting area. It was here that, back in the last century, the miners suddenly came

136

upon strata bearing abnormally rich ore. It was about 10 percent per weight of the soil, as opposed to 0.4 percent elsewhere in the area. The deposit was also unusual in that the uranium 235 isotope which normally occurs in natural uranium was almost entirely absent. This discovery, of course, led to considerable interest and study, resulting in the conclusion that you are looking at the remains of a natural nuclear reactor."

There were appreciative mumblings from the dozen or so persons before us. I moved nearer to the rail for a better look. It was not especially impressive—a big, rocky pit, scarred, gouged, gravelly at the bottom.

Fitting. A place like this perhaps, where the Galilean went to be tempted. . . . Is this irony necessary, new Lord? You have wrested the earth from its keepers to throw it away. . . . It is another world you claim to lead them to. . . . You care no more for the green, the brown, the gold, the glades, the glens, than this dry, hot place of rock and sand . . . and of death. What is death to you? A gateway . . .

". . . It was a spontaneous fission process which ran for over a million years," the guide went on. "We still have no idea as to what set it off in the first place. Nor can we say what genetic effect it may have had on local life forms. It could well have been quite spectacular. The resultant mutants could have spread themselves throughout the world in those millions of years since it burned itself out. Who knows what plant or animal, common today, owes its origin to the atomic pile which once smoldered here? Makes you stop and think." He paused to grin. "The world might be an entirely different place than it is today, were it not for the rocks from this strange hole in the ground—the only natural atomic pile of which we have ever found evidence."

"Didn't mankind originate in Africa?" one of the tourists asked.

"Many researchers believe so," answered the guide.

"Then could it be possible that this place had something to do with it?"

The guide smiled again. I could see in his mind that

he had heard the same question countless times before. He began a measured reply.

"Of course no one can say for certain. But it is curious that . . ."

I tapped Quick's shoulder.

"I get the idea," I said. "Let's go."

He nodded, and we turned away and made our way back to the transportation stand.

"It was very interesting," he said. "But I wonder why she wanted us to see it?"

"My benefit," I said. "I had never heard of it."

"Really? I thought everyone had."

"My education is still pretty limited. She wanted to prove something to me."

"What?"

"That something I was already positive I had experienced was not just some sort of psychic plant, from back when she was my therapist—and that the story I heard under those circumstances had something like a factual basis. All this, in case I started to wonder. All right. I believe her. Damn it!"

"I am afraid I do not understand."

"That's okay. I guess I am really talking to myself. Quick, I'm scared."

"Of what?"

"That guy last night. They have human agents. I had not known about that until just recently. I should have guessed as much, but I didn't."

"Who has human agents? What are you talking about? You are going too fast for me."

"She never told you about the enemy?"

"No."

"She must know, if she knows the man I am looking for, knows as much else as she does. . . ."

"Then I guess she just did not see fit to tell me."

"Well, I do. I've got to tell someone."

I did not finish till we were back in town, back at the hotel. When I had, he shook his head. He lit a cigarette.

"Damnedest story I ever heard," he said.

"You don't believe it?"

"I do believe it. Wish I didn't. It makes a kind of ghastly sense. I do not understand what you are going to do to help the situation, though."

"Neither do I."

"Let's get packed and go eat. Then we had better find that airfield."

I nodded, and we did.

Night. Crossing the Congo in a small flier. Quick, me, a nameless pilot. The only light in our small box in the sky came from the dim dials of the instrument board and the glow of Quick's cigarette. We flew low. I watched the night sky and communed with my other selves. Slowly, I began to appreciate what might lie ahead.

"Something out there," Quick said.

He was looking to the left, his head tilted slightly downward. I unfastened my belt and rose partway from my seat to follow his gaze.

Sixteen or seventeen meters off and three down, a dark shape paced us. Its form was birdlike, but its wings did not move. It was perhaps a meter in length, and half again that from wingtip to still wingtip. I probed, but no infrahuman awareness met my scrutiny.

"That is no bird," Quick said, "at this speed, gliding that way."

"You are right," I told him.

He swung his side window farther open and rested his left forearm on the frame. He lay his right wrist atop it, and I saw that he had the pistol in his hand. I raised my voice to be heard over the wind.

"I do not think that is going to do any good."

"Let's find out."

He fired. There came a bell-like tone.

. . . *And I remembered the beast, driving in among the rocks, its horns slashing toward my belly. Inches short, it began to throw its weight from side to side, spatulate legs continuing their paddlelike movement, body ringing like a great bell each time that it struck against the stone. I could smell the dried brine.* . . .

"Didn't faze it," he said.

The pilot shouted a query, and Quick yelled, "Take it up."

We began to climb.

"No good," he muttered half a minute later.

"Quick, I do not think we are going to get rid of it," I said, "and it has not made any hostile moves."

He nodded and put the pistol away. He adjusted the window.

"Just an observer, huh?"

"I think so."

"Ours or theirs?"

"Theirs."

"What makes you think so?"

"It reminds me of something else—from long ago."

"And we should just let it be?"

"I think we have no choice."

He sighed. He lit another cigarette.

It followed us that entire night, all across the Congo. The first time we landed—a fueling stop at a primitive field, used mainly by smugglers, according to our pilot's thinking—the bird-thing simply circled overhead.

Aloft again, it took up its position once more. I slept for a time, and when I awoke we were over Uganda and a pale light was infusing the sky before us. I was still feeling fatigued but was unable to return to sleep. Our escort was a piece of the night, reflecting nothing of the morning's illumination. Each time we fueled it waited, joining us again when we resumed flight.

The full light of day flashed upon Lake Victoria. I searched ahead with my mind. Something. For a moment, I detected something bright and powerful, and then it was gone. I ate a sandwich and drank some tea. We crossed into Kenya, kept going. I thought back to whatever it was I had touched upon, and I began to grow nervous. Toward what were we rushing and what would be expected of me? In myself I was nothing, possessed of no special skills beyond my TP abilities. Was this the desired quantity? Or would it be better to confront whatever lay ahead in the person of some greater individual I had been? I could reach out so easily to touch once again those minds. . . . But then, I had no way of knowing which to choose. I watched the land pass beneath us—green, brown, yellow. Quick had finally nodded and was breathing gently. The pilot's mind indicated that our next stop would be at the Somali coast, our destination.

The bird-thing left us when we disembarked at that final landing, streaking eastward, dwindling, gone. I was feeling faintly feverish, a combination of the fatigue and the tension, I supposed. It was a sunny afternoon, and we were near the center of a freshly cleared area. A new-looking hut stood across from us. Both the hut and a stack of fuel drums were concealed beneath thatched canopies. I sensed two presences within the structure—a mechanic and his assistant, who would shortly be checking over the flier and fueling it. Our pilot entered and spoke with them in Swahili. Neither knew what we were to do next.

"Quick, I don't feel so good," I said.

"I'd imagine. You don't look so good. How about a drink?"

"Okay."

I thought he meant water, but he produced a small flask from one of the many pockets in his bush trousers and passed it to me.

I took a long swallow of brandy, coughed, thanked him and passed it back.

"Have you any idea what we do now?" he asked.

I realized suddenly that I did. My tension, my physical distress, my anxiety, my curiosity and my desire were instantly fused into an aching from which I reached out, moving in the direction of the vanished shadowbird. I felt once again the presence I had touched upon earlier, and in that moment realized that it now lay upon me to make my own way. I turned east and began walking toward the sea, of which we had had a glimpse on the way down. Yes, it felt right to be doing that. There was some sort of easing of pressure as I moved.

Quick was beside me, reaching toward my shoulder.

"Hey! Where you going?"

"This way," I said, avoiding his hand. "Stay here. There is nothing more for you to do."

"The hell you say! I am your bodyguard till Lydia discharges me." He fell into step beside me. "Now, what happened?"

"I know where I must go."

"Great. You could have told me, though."

"It may be better if you do not accompany me."

"Why?"

"You could be injured."

"I'll take my chances. I have to be certain you get where you are going—all the way."

"Come on, then. I have warned you."

There was a trail through the brush. I followed it. When it turned right, I did not. By then the brush had thinned, however, and we were able to make steady progress. The way slanted gently downward for a time.

"Heading toward the water?" Quick asked.

"I think so."

"You said I could be injured. Can you be more particular as to the nature of the threat?"

"No. I do not know what it is. It is just a feeling that I have. They really only want me."

"Who are 'they'?"

"I haven't any idea now."

Walking. The way grew steeper. I continued to feel feverish, but I now regarded myself in an almost abstract fashion. It was as if, having hosted so many minds, my body might be something of a way station, a place where I, too, was but a passing fragment of the humanity come to temporarily inhabit it, ready to abandon it to another when my stay was done. I steered it over outcrops of shale, occasionally using my hands in steeper spots.

"Dennis, I think we ought to stop to rest," Quick said after a time.

"No. I have to go on."

"You are breathing hard and you've cut your hand. Sit down. There!" He indicated a flat-topped stone.

"No."

He seized me by the shoulders. I found myself seated on the flat-topped stone.

"Drink some water." He passed me a canteen. "Now let me see that hand."

He dressed my right hand as I drank. Then he lit a cigarette and readjusted his belt holster to place the pistol in a more accessible position.

"I cannot believe that Lydia wants you to get there in less than good shape."

"It doesn't matter, Quick. Something is drawing me toward it now, making me regret every moment I waste like this. It does not matter if I get there tired. It is my mind that is important."

"Never slight your body, Dennis. You might be capable of all manner of mental gymnastics—but these days everybody talks so much about psychosomatics that I think they sometimes forget it works the other way around. If you want that mind of yours in good shape for whatever lies ahead you will be a little kinder to the anatomy and psysiology that go along with it."

"I cannot look at it that way just now."

"Then it's a good thing I came along."

We rested for several more minutes. Then Quick ground out his cigarette and nodded to me. I got to my feet and continued down the slope. I decided against further thinking. My emotions were numb and I no longer trusted my intellect. I concentrated on moving in the direction which summoned me with greater authority with each step that I took. I felt that I was no longer in a position to judge anything, but that I could only respond to what was presented to me. Whether this feeling itself was a response planted in my mind long ago by Lydia, or whether it was a totally appropriate reaction dictated by the physiology of survival I would probably never know.

The man hurries toward the meadow his party had crossed earlier. There had been a rocky knoll in its midst. . . .

He breaks into the open, running toward the hillock. From the thunder at his back, he is already aware that

*he will be unable to attain a sufficient vantage in time
to roll rocks down upon his pursuer.*

*He races toward a stony cleft, slips within it and
turns, crouching.*

The ground leveled off and we entered an area of
heavier brush. I located a trail, though, and we continued to make good progress. Perhaps twenty minutes
later, the foliage began to thin. At the same time, the
trail took a downward turn. We moved along until it
lost itself in the place where the brush dwindled to low
shrubbery and dry grasses. I still knew the way—better
than ever, for the strength of the summons continued
to grow—and I bore toward my left through an area of
sandier soil.

At length, we came to a hill and climbed it. From its
top, the sea was now visible, perhaps two miles distant,
green, sparkling.

Old.

The sea and this land, both.

I halted for a moment. It was the first time in my
life that the concept of vast ages struck me in just that
fashion. I suppose that my youth had something to do
with it. I had not existed long enough for the accumu-
lation of much personal history; consequently, I had
never reflected on the nature of duration as it applied
to me. As for those other lives I had touched during
my stay on the moon, the time spans which separated
us meant nothing when I could simply reach them as I
would call to a friend across a room. But this, this
prospect of rock and water, told me of geological chro-
nology in a way that even the view from the moon had
not. There, though I had seen the world *in toto*, bright
and lovely, I was too removed, too distant—too new to
the fact of seeing, perhaps—to look upon it as more
than a celestial artifact, cunningly wrought, existing in
the moment. And the moon itself, about/above me . . .
The static character of its airless surface, its mo-
tionlessness . . . It was a place where time was frozen,
process outlawed. . . .

And so the present vista made me think for the first
time, as my own thoughts, of the age of the world, of

its—lifetime. It made me think of all the tamperings with its life systems. And suddenly, in the play of the afternoon light upon water and this small corner of Africa's old estate, I saw my movement as something more than a compulsion. More, even, than a duty; though this, too, was of it. There rose in me the desire to do anything to preserve the ancient land and waters of my world against the planned obsolesence which had pursued them across countless afternoons—perhaps since the stoking of the now-dead reactor in Moanda. I realized, too, that I might not be what I am but for that ancient device. Yet, I had to be more than a windup toy. We all did, or life was meaningless. The dark man had told Van Duyn that the one answer to the course of human affairs, the answer no longer taken seriously—the teleological one—was correct. We had had a rule of determinism forced upon us. Only by breaking it, somehow, could we save our home, our lives. . . .

Whatever was asked of me, that now was my desire.

But tell me . . . Is anything ever done?

I headed down the hill, my eyes on the coastline. The beach was dun, rock-strewn; the sea drew creamy curves along its length. I smelled it now in the racing wind. Dark birds circled, slid above its waves. A finger of land almost touched the water below and to my left. I could not see beyond it; to where my course led me.

Fifteen minutes later, we trod the sand and the pebbles, moving to round that prominence. I could hear the calls of the birds, the splash of the waves, feel the cold force of the winds. . . .

The wind blows on, the world goes as it will, coursing the same route it would have taken had I never been at all. . . .

The force that was drawing me grew into vision, so that I saw the dark man standing facing the sea before we passed the rocky hill and beheld him with our eyes.

He knew that I was there, though he did not look in my direction. I could sense this awareness within his consciousness. Most of his attention, however, was focused on something farther east, beneath the waters.

Quick halted, his hand upon the butt of his weapon.

"Who is it?" he asked.

"The dark man," I said, "who spoke with Van Duyn. The ancient enemy of our ancient enemies. He who was gored."

The man turned and regarded us. He was of medium height. He had on shorts and unlaced tennis shoes. He wore a medallion about his neck. He leaned upon a lance of dull metal. I felt the full force of his attention shift toward me.

Dennis Guise. This is the time and the place. Things are ready. Are you?

Yes. But I do not understand.

He smiled across the ten or twelve meters that separated us. Neither of us moved to draw nearer.

. . . The vision of Van Duyn as he looked at the East River, as he looked out across the silent city . . .

I have seen. I remember. It is not this which I do not understand.

Quick caught my eye.

"What is happening?" he asked.

I raised my hand.

Quick nodded.

"I hear him," he breathed.

They dwell out there, the man indicated, gesturing with his spear, *beneath the waters. I come to this place periodically, to speak with them. As always, I have been attempting to convince them that their plan is failing, that mankind is more complex, has become less responsive to their promptings than they had anticipated, that sufficient remedial action has been taken to thwart them, that something has been learned from all man's missteps, that it is time for them to concede the game and depart.*

Do they answer you? I asked.

Yes. They maintain the opposite.

How can such a matter be resolved?

By means of an example.

What am I to do?

You must go to them and let them examine you.

146

How will that win your case? I asked. *What can I show them?*

But even as I asked it, realization after realization swept over me. It was as if this dark stranger, rather than Lydia, were my only begetter, and that he had treated me as the enemy had treated the entire race, shaping my life—my illness, my recovery, the precise nature of each of my experiences—manipulating me to the extent necessary to produce just such a being as myself at this moment, in this place, so that he might give me to the enemy to examine in any way they saw fit, hopefully demonstrating that mankind had changed from the being of their original specifications, and that—as I now knew from my experience of history— the past is not lost to us, is not a bridge that has been burned leaving only ashes, but rather is an open way, that all of history is there to be explored, learned from, and even if they destroy me, more such as myself may arise at any time. He would offer me as a symbol, an example, showing that the race has learned and continues to learn from its mistakes.

You gave Van Duyn a choice, I told him.

How can I do it for you when I already know your answer?

I lowered my head.

The dice were loaded then, too.

There was no other way. There still is not.

I looked out at the waters, up at the sky, down at the beach. I might never see them again, I realized.

Where are they? I finally asked.

I will call them.

He turned away, facing the waters.

"And now?" Quick asked. "What is he doing?"

"Summoning my judges."

He placed his hand on his pistol.

"I don't like the sound of that."

"It must be."

"All right. Then what I do must be also, if they try to harm you."

"You must not interfere. You know what is at stake."

He did not answer, but jerked his eyes from mine and stared out over the waters. Even before I turned and looked I saw it in his mind.

A sphere with a mirror finish had broken the surface of the sea. As I watched, it advanced. I could not judge its size or distance accurately. Reaching out, I detected living presences within, of some order of thought which I could not approach. They were aware of my scrutiny and they gave me no more than this glimpse.

It came rolling in, gleaming, circular, enormous. It struck a sandbar or some obstruction, perhaps forty meters offshore, and maybe a quarter-mile north of where I stood. There it rested.

The entire affair was managed without a sound interposed among the wind and the waves, the cries of the birds. As I watched, an opening appeared on the shoreward surface of the globe and a ramp was slowly extruded, slanting down into the water, just as soundlessly as the vessel's arrival.

They have come. The rest is up to you.

I licked my lips, tasted salt, nodded. I took a step forward. Quick moved with me.

No, said the dark man, and Quick froze in his tracks, reminiscent of the audience we— I had seen at the General Assembly meeting, that day, both long ago and yesterday.

I continued on. I approached the dark man, passed him on the seaward side. He was as expressionless as I knew myself to be at that moment. He clasped my shoulder as I went by. That was all.

As I paced beside the lapping waves, I thought of Quick, immobile. It had to be that way. He would have taken a shot at anything that tried to touch me. We could appreciate that. It was so simple. . . . We . . . For suddenly it seemed that I was no longer alone. My mind had played some trick, reaching out unconsciously perhaps, in some peculiar fashion, so that it was as if I were simultaneously myself and one other. Somehow, Roderick Leishman was with me. I felt that if I turned around I would see him walking at my back.

I did not turn around. I continued, my eyes fixed on the globe, far ahead, wave-washed, spray-swept, laced by the flight of dipping, pivoting birds.

The birds . . . Their flight . . . I saw them as through a stroboscope, slowing, the details of each movement clearly recorded in my brain, ready at a moment's notice to be transferred to my sketchpad.

. . . And it was as if Leonardo da Vinci walked beside Leishman at my back.

We passed on, scuffing sand, seeing where the surf drew its lines . . . as it had that day, aye, near Syracuse, where we almost captured the calculus ages early.

Archimedes joined da Vinci and Leishman, as we moved on in this ancient place, this land still virtually untouched, still throbbing with the pulse of the clean elements, oh gods, and might it be that man could live in greater harmony with your bounty. . . . And Julian, Flavius Claudius Julianus, last of the old defenders, was with me, to be joined moments later by Jean Jacques Rousseau, staggering.

And as I walked, as at the head of an army, the others came, and I reached out across the bridge, no longer ashes, touching one by one, two by two, then dozens of the men I had been, filling myself with their presences—all of those who had been defeated in the name of man, great failures and small, suppressed men of learning, broken geniuses, talents cut short, twisted, destroyed—I was immersed within their number, but I was one of them: the switchboard, the contact, the point man. There was Leonardo; there, Condorcet; there, Van Duyn . . .

As I waded out into the surf, approaching the down-shot ramp, I made the final leap back, to become the dying god-king who will be resurrected to a sweet-smelling springtime, he whose sons and sons' sons have hunted the land since before the hills were made, he who had spoken with the powers beneath the sea, he who had summoned them here, he who stood now upon the beach with his spear upraised. I was the dark man, who bore all names.

Walking up the ramp, as in slow motion, we entered the darkened interior of the vessel, seeing nothing. But we could feel their presences, cold and powerful, scrutinizing the thing man had become. . . .

Walk. This way.

And we were guided. We felt them. We saw nothing.

Around the vessel, slowly, counterclockwise, we stepped, moving beneath the pitiless gaze of our makers. . . .

Time, somehow, meant nothing. We paraded before them. All of us they had thought destroyed. Back again. Moving through the darkness of their judgment.

And then there was light. Far ahead. We hesitated.

Keep walking, man.

We continued on in the direction of the light. As we drew near, we saw that it was a port, not unlike the one by which we had come in. Only . . . the day was waning now, the sun falling behind the rocky shoreline bluff to the west. I halted.

Keep going, man.

Is that all you have to say to me? After all this time? After all that has been done?

Goodbye.

I found myself moving once more, down the ramp, into the water, shoreward. I did not look back until I had reached the beach. When I did, the vessel was gone.

I found that I was shaking as I headed back to the spot where the dark man still stood. Somewhere along the way I lost my companions. Quick lay, apparently asleep, on the sand. He stretched and yawned as I approached.

"Come this way," the dark man said. "The moon is up. The tide is rising."

Quick and I followed him down the beach and retreated back along it. He moved a stone and dug beneath it with his spear. He uncovered a cache of supplies and proceeded to build a brushwood fire.

"What now?" Quick asked.

"Eat with me and wait with me," he said.

We did. The sun had gone away and the stars come out. The fire warmed us against a chill wind. A heavy moon silvered the waters.

Long into that night we waited. It was Quick who suddenly stood and pointed out over the ocean.

The moon, now westering, turned their surfaces to pale fire.

Like bubbles they rose from the sea and lifted into the air, climbing the night. I watched, losing count quickly, as they rose, climbed, vanished, rose, climbed, vanished, like strings of pearls losing themselves among stars.

"They are going!" Quick said.

"Yes," answered our companion.

"Will they try the same thing somewhere else?" Quick asked.

"Of course."

"But we have won? The world is ours once more?"

"So it seems, with no one to blame but ourselves for whatever follows."

For perhaps another hour we watched, until the sky was empty of them once again. Our companion was smiling in the firelight, when suddenly his expression changed and he clutched at the medallion he wore.

He was on his feet in an instant.

"What is it?" Quick asked.

"Get out of here! Now!" he shouted.

He scrambled to where his spear stood upright in the sand.

Then I heard it, a deep, hooting sound, rolling in over the waves, rising, becoming a whistle, vanishing somewhere above the audible. I was stricken, unable to move with the sudden clutch of fear that took me then. Reflexively, I reached out with my mind, but there was nothing there.

"Go! Get out!" he shouted again. "Hurry!"

At that moment, the sound came once again, much nearer, and some dark form rose from the waters and advanced toward us across the wide expanse of the beach. Quick dragged me to my feet and pushed me in the direction of the foothills. I stumbled forward, broke into a run.

Our companion was retreating also. When I glanced back, I saw streaks of moonlight upon a moving shape. It was long and supple; it appeared to be scaled. We departed the beach and began to climb. Behind us, the sound bellowed forth once more. It was coming at an extremely rapid pace, and in the moments of silence following its challenge I could hear a metallic clicking as it passed over stones, pebbles. Shortly, I felt a vibration within the ground.

We climbed. Our ancient oppressors had departed, but they had left this final doom for their greatest enemy. I saw this within the dark man's mind.

We reached the place where the grasses began, and then low shrubbery. I hoped that the slope might slow something of such obvious bulk as our pursuer. But its next blast was even louder than the previous. The ground was definitely shaking now. When I looked again, moonlight glinted on a great horned head and unnaturally crooked legs, splayed almost sideways, digging into the ground, propelling it through all obstacles. It was almost upon us.

The dark man swerved, moving away from us. It followed him, knocking down trees, dislodging rocks. Quick turned and pursued it across the slope. I heard his pistol firing. It rang like a bell with each shot as the rounds ricocheted from it.

The dark man turned to face it, bracing his lance against the slope. The beast rushed upon it, and I heard a grinding, rasping noise. The entire scene was, for a moment, frozen in the moonlight, like some awful statue: the beast had halted, the lance half-buried within it somewhere beneath the head, the dark man straining to hold it.

Then the head swung, once, and a horn caught the dark man somewhere low, throwing him far to the side. At that moment, it rang once more as Quick struck the back of that head with a large rock. It slumped then and lay still. Whether Quick's blow had done it or whether it was already finished, we would never know.

I rushed to the dark man's side. Moments later, Quick joined me, breathing heavily. Our companion was still alive, but he was unconscious. His side was very wet.

"Good God!" said Quick, tearing off his shirt, folding it, pressing it against the wound. "I think he's had it! There is no hospital anywhere near—"

"Leave him. Go. Get back to your flier. Never speak of this," came a familiar voice which I could not for the moment recognize.

When I turned, I saw that it was Lydia, coming down the slope.

"Your job is finished," she said. "Take the boy home, Quick."

"Lydia," he said, "we can't just go."

"There is nothing more for you to do here. Leave him to me. Go!"

I reached out with my mind. There was still life within the dark man, but it continued to wane.

"But—"

"Now!"

She gestured up the slope, and something about the way she did it made us turn that way.

"Come on, kid," Quick said. "Don't say anything else."

I went with him. He was right about not saying anything else. I could not have, even if there had been something to say. We walked, and I wanted to look back, but I was unable to do that either.

After a time, when we were higher and moving through heavier brush, passing among trees once more, I heard a sound like singing, from far away. I could not fully hear nor understand the words and I tried to listen with my mind.

. . . *Trees and mountains, streams and plains, how can this thing be?* I seemed to hear. *Rend yourselves, hide yourselves, spill yourselves over, weep . . .*

I— I staggered. For a moment, I seemed to be lying

there, bleeding, my head in her lap. Then the song was lost to me, there among the trees.

We hurried on, through the faded remains of the night.

About the Author

A former Secretary-Treasurer of the Science
Fiction Writers of America, Roger Zelazny
began writing professionally in 1962. He currently resides with his wife and son in Sante
Fe, New Mexico. His 16 published books
and 70 short stories have earned him several
Hugo and Nebula Awards, the highest hon-
ors given to writers of Science Fiction. Many
of his works have been translated into foreign
languages and one is currently being made
into a film. JACK OF SHADOWS and TO-
DAY WE CHOOSE FACES are his previous NAL books.

SIGNET Science Fiction You'll Enjoy